BARBARIAN'S REDEMPTION

RUBY DIXON

RUBY DIXON

Photo by: Sara Eirew Photographer

Cover Design by: Kati Wilde

This book is a work of fiction. I know, I know. Imagine that a book about big blue aliens is fiction, but it is. The names, characters, places, and incidents are products of the writer's imagination or have been used fictitiously and are not to be construed as real. Any resemblance to persons, living or dead, actual events, locales or organizations is entirely coincidental and would be pretty darn nifty.

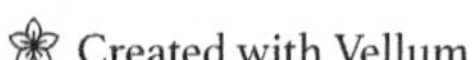

BARBARIAN'S REDEMPTION

For seasons, I have waited for her - my perfect mate.

In a tribe full of happy couples, I am alone. But I am not content to remain this way. There are no eligible unmated females left, so I will do whatever it takes to bring females back to our tribe...even if it means doing something wrong. Even if it means I must purchase my mate on the intergalactic black market. I will do anything to possess her, to claim her as my own.

But will my ruthless move turn my female against me before we ever meet? Can she ever forgive a male that bought her freedom?

1

ELLY

"Look alive, ladies," Gail says softly in the corner of her cell. "We've got company."

The other human slaves stand in their tiny cells, moving to the front bars to see. I know better. I've been a slave for a long time now, and buyers are never something to look forward to. Granted, being kept on a slave ship is just as bad, but at least it's a familiar sort of 'bad.' I can deal with familiar bad. It's the bad I don't know that terrifies me. But I've learned a lot in my ten years of being a slave. I don't get up. I push my filthy, matted hair forward to cover my face, just enough so I can still see out but they can't see my face. I hunch my shoulders and roll them slightly forward so my breasts look smaller and my collarbones more prominent.

I want to look as awful as possible so no one buys me. Especially so no one buys me as a playmate.

"What do you see, Gail?" The tall blonde holds on to her bars and presses her face between them. "Where?"

"At the far end of the hall," Gail murmurs, voice low and calm. Gail's our unofficial watchdog, since her cell's near the front of the long hall and she can see out one of the small windows into the next room. Gail's been here almost as long as I have, and she's the closest thing I have to a friend—or at least, she would be if I ever talked to anyone. "They're speaking with Big Cheese," Gail tells us.

A few cells down, the girl with the pink-dyed hair sobs. She's new and hasn't yet learned to hide her emotions. "A-are we going to get sold?"

"Maybe," Gail says. She puts her hands on the bars of her small cell and stands on her tiptoes, trying to peer out. "Y'all be quiet so I can listen."

The cages of humans go silent. We all want to know what Gail's hearing, even me.

Gail tilts her head, listening. She learned the alien language from her last master, she told me once when I realized she could understand them. He trained her so she would know what he asked for. Judging from her expression, he didn't ask for anything good. Not surprising. At this point, I'm used to terrible treatment. As far as owners go, these slavers aren't so bad. We get fed at least once a day, sometimes twice when they're feeling generous. I can stand up in my cage, though the tall blonde in the cage next to me can't. And so far no one's tried to have sex with me. All in all, I've had worse.

Which is why I'm uneasy that there are buyers here. This place isn't great, but there's worse out there. I know the others want to get away...but they're still so new. They don't know how bad it can be out there. I've had three owners in ten years. I know just how bad it can be.

"They're here to buy humans," Gail says after a moment. Her small hands are tight on her bars, and she tries to climb a little higher. "Saying something else, too, but I can't make it out. They don't speak any languages I know."

"What do they look like?" someone farther down the line asks. Might be Kate. "Do they look nice?"

"They're blue," Gail says. "And really, really tall. I see horns, too."

"Horns? Like devils?" the blonde next to me asks.

Gail steps back and waves a hand, indicating we should all be quiet. "They're coming!"

Immediately, everyone scurries to the backs of their cages. The blonde tries to cover her breasts with her tight curly hair, but it's not long enough. I watch as Gail folds her tiny body close, tucking her legs under her and crossing her arms over her chest. She's probably twice my age, but she's supple and lithe, her dark skin gleaming in the low light of the cellblock. Everyone's quiet, waiting.

There's a hiss of air, and then the door opens.

The first thing I notice is that they're not wearing masks when they enter, or the nose-clips that filter toxins out of the atmosphere. My first master made me wear one of them because the atmosphere he preferred was poisonous to humans. And a lot of the 'shoppers' that come through to gawk at humans wear masks over their breathing orifices for the same reason. They also usually don't buy, which means that these particular shoppers might be more than just browsing.

That worries me.

I watch them from under the curtain of my filthy hair. Gail's right; they're extremely tall, and it doesn't just seem that way because Gail's so tiny. They're taller than humans by at least a foot, and the horns make them seem even more imposing. Their bodies are big and muscular, their skin a denim shade of blue. They're strong. I'm starting to get scared. I hunch my shoulders a little more, doing my best to seem helpless. I'm a pro at being avoided. Heck, I've managed to be here for almost a year, so I'm hoping one of the other girls looks a bit more appealing than me. It's awful to think that way, but I don't have a choice.

There are two men eyeing the rows of cages, walking behind the slavemaster. The slavemaster is all smooth rolling words in his native tongue, gesturing at the line-up of the human cages. He must smell a sale, because he's especially oily today, all big hand motions and butt-kissing that's obvious even without knowing his language. The big blue men don't look especially thrilled at the sight of us. One of them seems to be older than the other, face lined and dark hair shot with gray, like Gail's. He peers in on my cage and then flinches backward at the sight of me, saying something. Probably worried about how unhealthy I look. The slavemaster murmurs something apologetic, and I can guess what he's saying. Turning 'she's mean' into 'she's got a lot of fire' or 'she needs taming' or something along those lines. These guys can spin anything. I can ask Gail later what they said, if she's still here. If I'm still here.

The younger one says something to the other and they seem to argue. He gestures, holding up fingers. Five. Then he points at our cages and makes another sweeping gesture. Oh no. Are they here to buy all five of us? There are five humans locked up, and I've never seen anyone leave with more than one girl. One of my old masters told me we were expensive pets, and I guess we are. That's why the slavemaster looks overjoyed at the conversation.

He really, really does want to buy all of us.

I feel sick to my stomach at the thought. I'm safe here. I'm not safe if I leave with these two blue aliens. These men look brutal, strong enough to snap Gail in half, or me, or even the big strapping blonde to the other side of my cage. If they're mean, it's going to be really bad for us. I have no misconceptions of what they expect when they purchase slaves, hence my protective layer of filth.

Normally, I skate through a purchasing round by the fact that I'm scrawny, underfed and filthy. No one gives me a second look when there's a plumper, more attractive female nearby. It's my defense mechanism. But if they buy all of us...it means they don't care how dirty or thin I am. They just need a lot of humans and they don't care what we look like.

The thought is terrifying. I've heard stories of some alien races that like to throw 'dining' parties and eat people. Is that what we're all being bought for? A feast?

Living in a cage isn't much of a life, but I don't want to die, either.

"It sounds like they want to take all of us with them," Gail whispers from her spot in her cage. "They're just haggling over the price. They want to pay less for you, Elly. Says you're not healthy."

I feel a tiny surge of hope at that. If I look too sick, maybe they can leave me behind.

The men continue to argue, and the older one keeps glancing over into my cell. The younger one argues and pulls out a bag, counting out the small squares that I know pass for intergalactic currency of some kind.

"The older one wants to leave you, but the younger one says their agreement was five. I don't know why they need five, they just keep saying that over and over again." Gail frowns to herself. "Says they promised something called a 'bek.' Do you know what alien race that is?" She looks over at me, her eyes dark, worry on her face.

I shake my head slowly, watching as the men count out money.

"Well, sounds like we're gonna find out."

The men pause, and the older one gestures at Gail and says something.

"Oh, hell no, you did not just call me old," she mutters under her breath. "He's trying to get a damn discount for you and me. Cheap-ass bastard."

Poor Gail. She sounds offended. I'm not. I want them to not be able to agree on a price. I want them to leave me behind.

The men continue talking for a moment more, and then the younger one makes an angry sound and hands over his entire bag of credits to the slavemaster, who quickly pockets it. The older one just shakes his head, his mouth flattening into a firm line, and spits out a few words. I catch a glimpse of fangs. Oh Jesus, fangs too? I fight the rising panic that I'm feeling, because this can't be happening. I can't be sold to someone this big and scary. I can't.

The slavemaster utters a few pleased words, and then heads over to the far end of the hall of cages, unlocking Gail's first. He talks all the while, pulling a few force-collars off the wall and offering them to the elder of the two buyers. The one says something to Gail, and she taps the translator in her ear.

"I can hear just fine, and I heard what you said. All these other girls don't speak your language, though."

He puts a finger to his ear and then says something to the younger male. A moment later, he speaks again. "Can you understand me?" His English is thick and heavily accented but understandable.

I hear someone else in the cages gasp.

Gail nods slowly. "Yes. Thank you."

"The collars will not be necessary, will they? I assume you are as civilized as the rest of your people?"

"If you mean will we run away, I can't speak for the others, but I won't. Where are you taking us?" She crosses her arms under her small breasts, standing tall and proud despite her diminutive height.

"Can you take us home?" Kate cries out, hope in her voice. The other girls murmur, and I feel a stab of excitement in my belly.

The older one shakes his head. "Your planet is off limits. Even purchasing you is taboo. I risk enough buying you from this flesh peddler." He glances over at the slavemaster, who's beaming and giving him approving looks. "I am purchasing you for a friend."

It sounds so reasonable, but I grow cold. My very first master, the one that kept me in his private zoo, gave me to his 'friend.' Just because he says he doesn't want us for himself doesn't mean we're not in danger.

We're still slaves. We're still not free.

"Come," the older one says. "We're wasting fuel with every moment we idle here. I want to get you deposited and then I can be done with this business."

The younger one nods, a nervous look on his face. "I'd like to get out of here before anyone records that our ship is here. I don't like the thought of spending the rest of my life in a Ktharian jail."

The elder one grunts. "Let us go, then." He nods at the slavemaster, and Gail's cell is opened. She steps out calmly, waiting, and looks over at me.

It's gonna be okay, she mouths and gives me a small thumbs-up. So confident. She doesn't know, though. None of them do. We don't have any idea of what's coming ahead. It could be an utter nightmare.

I'm not going down without a fight, though. So when they open my cage, I flinch back, huddling in the corner. If I thought snarling would do any good, I'd try that, too. The slavemaster sighs and says something to the others in his strange language.

"Get out here already," the younger one says, impatience stamped on his face. "I know you can understand me. Come on. We don't have a lot of time."

Does he think I'm going to go with him willingly? After what I've seen and lived through? He's just my newest captor. I'm never going to go easily, because it doesn't matter. You can be the most willing slave in the world and someone will always want to hurt you just because you're property. So I remain huddled against the wall and ignore him, keeping my face angled down so my hair can shield the fear on my face. I hate letting them see I'm afraid.

The slavemaster offers a collar, but the older one declines. Now they're all frowning at me. Like I'm the problem.

I hug my arms tight to my chest, keeping against the wall. And when the big one comes in, my fear and instincts take over. He reaches for me with one big hand...

So I bite it.

He jerks away, and as he does, it knocks me backward. My head hits the wall, and I'm dazed. Ears ringing, I gaze blearily up at them as the slavemaster steps in and gives me a whack with the shock-stick. Electricity shoots through my veins, and I can't breathe, every muscle in my body screaming to a halt. I shiver, and my mouth falls slack as I collapse to the floor. I can feel the drool sliding down my cheek, but I can't close my mouth. I can't do anything.

As if this is no big deal, the slavemaster steps next to my fallen body and calmly snaps the collar around my neck, then pats my cheek. Good dog.

I hate him. So much.

"Oh, Elly. Be careful," Gail says in a soft voice. "Don't get started on the wrong foot, honey." Then, louder, she says, "Elly's had some bad owners in the past. She doesn't trust much."

"She bit me," the older one says, voice stiff with anger. He cradles his enormous hand like I did real damage. Please.

I feel a little trickle of fear at that. Gail's probably right. I need to calm down. To go quietly. But every bone in my body won't let me give in. I can't do this. I can't just go with them like I'm happy to be property.

To be a good dog. Fuck that.

So when the slavemaster barks the word that I know means 'get up,' I test my muscles. They're working again, and I crawl slowly to my feet. They're watching me, the slavemaster with a benevolent but annoyed expression on his face that fills me with helpless anger. I know I shouldn't, but I can't help myself —I leap forward and bite him. Just because I'm never going to be his good dog.

The blast of the shock collar knocks me unconscious.

When I wake up again a short time later, I'm in a strange, well-lit place. I immediately think of the old zoo, with its constant overhead lighting and the calls of exotic birds a few cages away. I blink and look around, surprised to see a horned blue female waving a scanner over me.

"If you try to bite me, I'm going to put you back under and surgically remove all your teeth," she says in a dry voice. Her hands are wrinkled, her face lined, and she doesn't look friendly. "Got it?"

I pull my legs up tight against my body and huddle on the table I'm sitting on. I eye the room, looking for the familiar, but I'm here alone. The other humans aren't anywhere to be found, and I don't recognize this place.

The blue woman finishes running a scan on me. "You're dehydrated and malnourished. I'm going to give you a shot that will replenish some of the missing electrolytes and provide some vitamins, but you need to make sure you're eating enough."

I just stare at her, hugging my knees closer.

"Right. They said you weren't a talker. This makes my job so fun, doesn't it?" She shakes her head and stares down at an electronic pad, tapping out commands. "You have intestinal parasites, too. Can I give you something to kill those, or do you want to keep them?"

Keep them? Who on earth would keep a parasite? I stare at her.

She shrugs. "I've heard of weirder. Okay, well, I'm going to give you a pill that will kill them. You can choose to take it or not." She moves to another wall panel and taps a few buttons. A couple of pills slide into a small metal cup, plinking as they do. "I would also recommend a good scrub and a de-lousing since you're pretty keffing filthy, but that's just me." The woman turns and holds the cup out to me, waiting.

I want to knock it out of her hand, but...I also don't want intestinal worms. I hesitate and then grab the pills, shoving them into my mouth and swallowing quickly.

"All right. That wasn't so hard." She gives me a brisk look and puts her pad away. She taps her wrist and speaks into it, changing languages. I can't make out what she's saying, but a moment later, the door to the bare, strange room I'm in opens up, and it's the younger blue guy.

He waves at me. "Follow, please."

I glance between him and the female. I'm not sure I want to go with him. The female is taller than I am, and leaner, but I have more of a chance to take her down than him. The male's easily twice my size.

"I wouldn't try it," the woman says. "I didn't take the shock collar off you." Her smile is thin and unamused. "I'm not stupid."

I reach up and sure enough, the awful collar is still around my neck. I feel another burst of helpless anger. I'd growl at them if I thought it'd do any good. With this thing on, though, they can disable me with the touch of a button. I hate them. I hate it.

I hate these blue people that pretend to be nice but it doesn't reach their eyes. It's like they're going through the motions of being polite but there's no real caring there.

The male gestures at the door. "Come on. I'm not going to ask you again."

I slide off the table and get to my feet, and I notice I'm wearing a thin paper gown of some kind, like in a doctor's office. It's the first piece of clothing I've had in almost a year, and it feels weird against my skin. Makes me feel itchy, too, and I realize just how dirty I am.

Doesn't matter, though. I'm staying dirty for now. Dirty's safe. No one wants to touch dirty.

The big horned male makes another impatient gesture at the door, and I hastily move forward, my steps wobbling. I feel a little lightheaded, and my head throbs. I step into a shadowy, unfriendly looking hallway that seems made entirely of metal. It reminds me of something from a spaceship movie. My captor grabs a small bundle from a shelf and then gestures that I should follow him.

I do, because I don't know if I have any other options. Not with the shock collar on. I don't mind the occasional slap with the shock-stick because they're mild, and a lot of the time, it's worth it. Bite the slavemaster? Totally worth the shock. Slap food out of an asshole guard's hand? Totally worth the shock. But the shock collar isn't mild. I've seen a big lizard-man slave have his brains melted and dribble out his nose after being zapped with the shock collar too many times. After that, I learned to fear the collar.

Fear's a powerful motivator for a slave.

The man leads me down a few twisting hallways and then taps on a wall panel. A door slides open, and inside I see the other humans. They're all huddled together in a room the size of my old bedroom back on Earth. Everyone is wearing paper gowns and hugging blankets around their shoulders. The male hands me the bundle—probably my blanket—and gestures that I should join the others. "It's going to take about two days for us to get to our destination. You lot need to stay here and be quiet. We'll bring you food. That door through there's the facilities." He points at a narrow cubby off to one side.

Gail pats the open spot next to her, and I move closer. "Are you taking us to Earth?" Gail asks, calm confidence in her voice. She's brave in her own way.

The male snorts. "No. Told you that. Earth's off limits. I don't know how they managed to stealth into the zone to grab you guys, but we'd be tapped on a radar and imprisoned for sure. You're not going back. We're taking you somewhere else."

One of the other girls—pink-haired Brooke—starts to cry. Kate hugs her close and rubs her shoulder, and there's worry in their faces.

Gail frowns. I can tell the news makes her feel bleak, but I'm not surprised. I knew years ago that I'd never see Earth again. It'll take her and the others some time to get used to the idea. "Then where are you taking us?"

"Somewhere else," he repeats, being vague. "The people there are nice."

"Are they human?"

He looks uncomfortable, then steps out of the doorway, about to leave. "I have work I need to do. Like I said, someone will be by with a meal in a few hours. Be quiet and try not to make too much noise."

"Clothing?" Gail asks as the door starts to slide shut. "And what if we—" He's gone before she can finish the sentence, though, and she mutters a string of curses. "From one holding pen to another," she says with a shake of her head. "Un-fucking-real."

"At least we can stretch," the tall blonde says. But she doesn't look thrilled.

I don't blame her. No beds, no clothes, and food dropped off as long as we're 'quiet'? They're not treating us like people. They're treating us like inconvenient pets. Been there, done that. People don't mind a pet as long as it doesn't cause too much trouble.

When they do, you find a new owner.

But I have a paper dress, and a blanket, and I'm with the others. In some ways, this is better than the last place, and in some ways it's worse. Until the other shoe drops and the real terrible things happen, it's best to enjoy the quiet. I unwrap my blanket and then lie down, my head throbbing with pain.

We have two days until we're handed off to our new masters. Two days before the world changes again.

I'm going to enjoy this blanket until then.

2

BEK

Every morning, as I always do, I rise with the dawn. I get up, dress, nudge Harrec with my boot because he snores loudly enough to wake a scythe-beak in the brutal season, and grab my weapons. I head out of the small hut I share with the other unmated hunters and stretch in the brisk morning air. I am the first one awake, and I glance around before heading off to my secret hiding place, where I have my secret box stashed. I head into the canyon, close to the dirt-beak nests, and look for the telltale outcrop of three rocks jutting out from the wall. I head for it, glance around to see if anyone else has followed me, and then drop to my knees, digging.

Every morning, I check the box for the red flash I am told will signal the ship's return. Every day, it is quiet and lifeless.

Today, though, I can see the flash even before I pull it free from its hiding spot buried under the snow. I cradle it in my hands, watching it flash the bright red I was promised, and I feel a surge of hope.

They did not lie.

They are coming back with humans.

Several moons ago, Mardok and his people arrived here. It was shocking to see people that were not of my tribe. Mardok and his 'ship' came from our homeworld, where our ancestors came from many, many generations ago. Cap-tan and Trakan and Niri were polite, but it was clear they did not understand the sa-khui life or why we would choose to stay here on our world instead of returning to the stars with them.

Mardok stayed, though. The ship left, and Mardok remained behind to mate with Farli, claiming the last eligible unmated female in our tribe. I am not upset about this—Farli is as a little sister to me, and I am happy she has found a mate that brings her joy.

But even so, I feel loneliness gnawing at my spirit. There are no females to mate. I will never have a family and a hearth of my own unless I wait patiently for one of the female kits in the tribe to come to adulthood.

And I am not a patient hunter.

So I asked Cap-tan and Trakan to bring humans here, humans they find that have been taken from their home, like Shorshie and the others. Humans that will be sold to bad men. I want them brought here so they can be mates to the men in our tribe. So we can give them a good life and make kits with them. So we can be lonely no longer.

Cap-tan and Trakan promised to bring us females because I showed them the cave-ship that brought Mah-dee and Li-lah and let them take a box of small, shiny squares that they were very excited about. They promised that because I had helped them, they would help me. And because they promised, they gave me a shiny square to wear on my wrist. It will blink red, they told me, when their ship returns to our planet. I am to watch it daily, and when it blinks, they will bring humans for us.

I was not entirely sure they would ever come back. I could tell that neither Cap-tan or Trakan liked the idea of bringing humans to my world. They said it was very bad to be found buying humans, but in the end they wanted the box of shiny chips more than they cared. I watch the slow blink of the wrist-square in wonder and elation. I have never been able to wear it. I have had to hide it, because no one in the tribe knows of the deal I have made except for Vaza. I am not sure that my chief, Vektal, would understand. He has a mate and two kits at his hearth. He is content. Even before, he had affection from females.

He does not know what it is like to be without hope. But Vaza understands. He approves.

And he will want to go with me to greet the ship's return.

I wrap the wrist-square in a bit of fur and hide it in my loin-cloth. The strange stone is cold against my groin, even through the fur, but it is the only place I can carry it and ensure no one will see I have it. I force myself to walk calmly back to the village, gripping my spear with white knuckles.

Out on the other side of the valley, the cave-ship is returning. It will be carrying humans, and one of them might be my mate. I feel a stab of nervousness. I was not a good pleasure-mate to Claire, and she left my furs. What if I am not good at being a mate to another female? What if I ruin things again? The thought eats at my mind.

I do not like the thought of offending another mate. It took many seasons for Claire to look at me as a friend again. I cannot imagine what it would be like if we had resonated.

But perhaps I am creating trouble where there is none. Perhaps I will not resonate to one of these females at all. The thought is a depressing one, and I banish it instantly. I will not allow myself to think such things, not while there is hope.

I return to the village and duck inside the hut I share with the others. Harrec continues to snore in his furs, oblivious to the morning sunlight. Taushen is gone, but Vaza is rising and Warrek is stirring. I grab the pack I normally take hunting with me and move to Vaza's side, then give him a meaningful look.

The elder straightens immediately, excitement flicking in his eyes. "Today?"

"Hmm?" Warrek asks, glancing over at us.

"Nothing," I say sharply. "Come hunt with me today, Vaza." I stress his name and give him a stern glance that indicates he should keep quiet. "Meet me outside when you are ready."

He flings himself from his furs, racing for his things. I ignore Warrek's look of surprise—he will understand later.

When I have a mate curled up at my side, resonating to me, her belly full of my kit, I will endure the chief's anger without fear. Nothing is worse than having no mate. Nothing. Whatever punishment he gives me for going behind his back, I will take.

Even if it means exile. If she is with me, I do not care where I go. My mate. She is close. I feel a need so intense it makes my chest clench.

Vaza stumbles out of the hut a scarce moment later, one leg barely in his leggings. He is hitching his belt at his waist and drops a boot as he rushes forward. "They are here?"

I scowl at him, clenching a hand tight around my spear. "Do not be so obvious," I grit. "The others will see and be curious."

He straightens, stuffing his leggings through his belt and then hitching it tight at his waist. He has an expression on his face that looks much like Claire's little Erevair when he must be calm and wait for a present—stoic yet desperately excited underneath.

Part of me resents his excitement. Vaza had a mate once, and a son. They both died in a terrible hunting accident long before the khui-sickness, and he has been alone ever since. He wants a mate and company, but any fertile female will surely resonate to one of the males who has never had a mate. He might very well be left alone once more.

I try not to think such depressing thoughts. Cap-tan and Trakan will bring enough females for all of us, surely. I watch impatiently as Vaza laces up his boots, and then grunt approval as he hikes over to me. "Let us go before anyone else notices." I feel as if we are being very obvious in our sneaking away.

"Bek!" calls out a tiny voice.

And just like that, I decide I can wait a few moments. I turn and kneel, smiling at the kit that races up to me, his little play spear in hand. "Erevair. Where is your mother?"

Claire's son is smaller than a full sa-khui kit would be. He is a pale blue—a cross between his mother's pale skin and sa-khui—but the unruly, floppy mane on his head is all his father. He blinks his big blue eyes up at me. "Feeding Relvi. Where are you going?"

"Hunting," I tell him.

"Can I go with you? Can we catch dirt-beaks?"

I chuckle and shake my head. I took the kit with me the other day to get dirt-beak nests, and he was so impressed by the birds that I caught a few of them with my hands, just to show off and make him laugh. It does not matter that Erevair is not my son—I love him as if he were my own. "I will take you another day."

The little one squints up at Vaza, not sure if he should pout or not. "Are you taking him dirt-beak hunting?"

"We are hunting something else," Vaza teases.

I shoot him an irritated look. If he hints what we are doing, Erevair will tell Claire. "We are very busy and must be going, Erevair. What would you like for me to hunt today?"

"Quill-beast!" He rubs his belly in an exaggerated motion that makes me laugh.

"I will bring one back for your mother's fire," I promise him, ruffling his mane. "Now go and tell her, and we will be off." We can stop by a cache and I can get a quill-beast from the frozen storage to appease him. There is enough time in this day, I should think.

As Erevair waves and races off again, Vaza just shakes his head. "You are soft on that one."

I get to my feet and head toward the far end of the crevasse, toward the pulley. "I am fond of all the kits."

"But especially fond of that one."

I say nothing, because I do not disagree. Though Claire is no longer my pleasure-mate, we are friends once more. I have spent many nights at her fire with her and her mate, Ereven.

And while I help my sister Maylak with her kits when I can, there is something special about Erevair. Perhaps I see him as the son I should have had, if I had resonated to Claire.

Of course, Claire and I would have been miserable as resonance mates. But sometimes I still wonder if it would have been different. I suppose I will always wonder as long as I am unmated and alone.

I glance over at Vaza, suddenly impatient. "Let us go quickly now."

He gives me an eager nod, and it takes all that I am not to sprint out of the village at the fastest of speeds.

By the time the twin suns are high in the sky, we have skirted around the large valley that holds our village's crevasse. The weather is clear and looks as if it will hold all day. The hills are full of wildlife, and I manage to spear a fresh quill-beast that we flush out of a snowdrift as we walk.

Surely this is a good sign of things to come.

In the distance, I can see the ugly, ungainly hulk of the cave-ship that belongs to Cap-tan and the others. It hovers slightly off the ground, which is strange to see given that it has no wings. It lands as we approach, and as I watch, the side opens up, a staircase descending. I remember this strangeness from when we visited before, though the sight of it is still unnerving. Trakan appears in the hole in the side of the cave-ship and raises a hand in greeting.

"Hey, man. Hurry it up," he calls out as we approach. "Captain says we're behind schedule for our next run, so we can't stay for long."

Vaza and I jog to meet him, and I climb the stairs, clasping his arm in greeting. "You returned."

"Would have felt like a keffing bastard if we didn't," he says with a grin. "Do you have any idea how many credit chits you gave us?"

I do not even know what a credit chit is. I shrug.

He greets Vaza and then gestures for us to follow him. "Come on. Captain's on the bridge and declined to say hello. Wants to keep out of the 'exchange' as much as possible. I think he wants to limit his culpability if we get caught."

"Caught?" I ask, stepping through the hole into the cave-ship. As in the past when I entered, a blast of heat hits me, as if a dozen fires are quietly burning out of sight. They do not like the cold, and their home is chokingly warm. I immediately begin to sweat, but I can endure the heat. It does not matter at all.

"Yeah, like I told you, humans are from a Class-D planet." He looks momentarily annoyed at my ignorance. "We get caught with them and it breaks all kinds of keffing treaties. I'll have to spend the rest of my days being bottom bunk in a backwater prison. No thank you."

I grunt at his words. "But you do have humans with you? Female humans?"

"That we do, my friend. Our debt to you will be officially paid." Trakan saunters down the corridor of the cave-ship. "After this, we have never seen each other before. Understand?"

"Of course." I just want to see the humans. I wipe sweat from my brow, and I do not know if it is from the heat or my nerves. Next to me, Vaza looks twitchy. "Where are they?"

"Right this way." He pauses in front of a wall and taps a few glowing buttons. "Had Niri run medical checks on them, and they all are in relatively good health. Some of 'em aren't the most pleasant creatures, but that's your problem, not mine."

The door opens, and Trakan steps aside so Vaza and I can enter. I step forward, my heart pounding. There are five small forms curled up in pale blankets. They sit up as we enter, and as I watch, they huddle together, gazing at us with frightened, dark, human eyes.

I look at each one, waiting for it. Waiting for that moment that resonance will strike. *Show me my mate,* I demand to my khui. *Pick one to resonate to.*

The one closest to me has a bright pink mane and large teats. She shivers and moves closer to her friend as I gaze in her direction. The friend is tall for a human—almost the size of a sa-khui female—and has a mane so pale it looks like tufted snow. She would make a good mate, I think. Beside her is a smaller one with golden skin, tilted eyes, and a black mane that brushes against her shoulders. She looks small, I decide. Fragile. Perhaps better for Taushen, because he has a gentle grip with delicate tools. Next to her is an even smaller female, so slight that she looks almost childlike. Her skin is a dark, rich color like Tee-fah-ni, and her hair is a tight cap of gray against her round scalp. She has wise eyes and narrows them at me, as if she does not approve.

But Vaza sucks in a breath at the sight of her. "They have sent an older female?" He puts a hand to his chest. "She must be mine."

Perhaps so. I did not ask Trakan if the humans were of a kit-bearing age. Perhaps I should have. I glance at the last human, buried underneath her blanket. She is the worst looking of the ragged bunch. Filthy, pale, underfed—if she were a dvisti, I would not even hunt her for meat. Her eyes are dark, and her face is so small and narrow that she seems nothing but eyes and a mess of filthy mane that hangs in her face.

Ugh.

I fight a surge of disappointment. Not only is my khui silent, but these humans are...not what I expected. One that is possibly too old to bear kits, two small and so fragile I would be afraid to touch them. That leaves the white-maned one and her pink friend. I eye the pink one's teats again. She has a good body for a human, but she is still crying, and that fills me with frustration.

"They're a little skittish." Trakan nods at me, a sly grin on his face. "See anything you like?"

I tap my too-silent chest. "My khui will decide who is right for me."

But Vaza looks besotted. He stares at the older female, unable to tear his gaze away. "What is the dark one's name?" he asks in a reverent voice.

Trakan scratches his head, glancing at the females, and then shrugs. "Didn't ask."

I look at him incredulously. "You did not ask?"

He shrugs again. "Didn't seem important. They're not staying." He looks over at the humans and nods at the dark-skinned one. "Hey," he calls, switching to the human language. "What is your name?"

"Oh, so you finally decided to talk to us instead of just staring in the doorway with your buddies?" Her brows go up in that fascinating, mobile way that humans have.

"You are the most beautiful human I have ever seen," Vaza breathes. I roll my eyes. Vaza falls in love quickly, it seems.

"Hmmph." She holds her blanket a little tighter to her body. "Well, I've seen better-looking aliens than you."

This one reminds me too much of Leezh.

"Just tell him your name," Trakan says, impatient. "These guys are your new masters."

A chorus of muffled gasps meets that announcement. The pink-haired one begins to cry again. The filthy one seems to shrink back against the tiny, mouthy one. None of them look thrilled.

"So you bought us, huh?" The angry one's voice goes flat. "Well then, I guess you can just call us whatever you want, can't you?"

"It would give me great pleasure to hear your name," Vaza tells her, adoration in his tone. "I am called Vaza."

The female's gaze flicks back and forth between the three of us. "Gail," she says finally.

One of the hard-to-pronounce human names. "Sh-shair," Vaza tries.

"Gail," the human repeats.

"Shail." Vaza tries again.

"Gail," she ventures again. "Hard G."

Vaza's mouth puckers. "Ch-chaaail."

A flash of annoyance crosses her face but quickly disappears. "You know what? You wanna call me Chail, sugar, you do that."

Her voice is too sweet to be sincere, but Vaza looks pleased. He turns and gives me an encouraging smile.

Poor fool. I nod at the other girls. "Names?"

The pink one looks at Chail. She sniffs and hiccups before answering. "Buh-Brooke."

I nod. That name is easier. "Buh-Brukh."

The females all frown up at me. "No, just Brooke," the pink one says, and flinches back. "But you can call me Buh-Brooke if you want."

"I'm Kate," says the one with the cloud of hair. Next to her, the tiny golden one says, "I'm Summer."

There is a pause. I look over at the filthy one, waiting for her to say her name. She just hugs her knees and stares at me from the curtain of her hair.

"This is Elly," Chail says after a moment, and gestures at the female sitting next to her, careful not to touch her. "Elly doesn't like to talk."

"Does her tongue not work?" I remember that Rokan's mate Lilah could not hear for many seasons, until the cave-ship fixed it for her.

"She just doesn't like talking," Chail answers for Ell-ee, who remains silent.

There is a foul smell in the room, and I suspect it is coming from one human in particular. "She does not like bathing, either, it seems."

"Elly's had a hard time," Chail says and moves forward protectively, careful not to touch Ell-ee but putting her body in front of her.

"So hard that she cannot use soap-berries?" I snort.

Chail gives me an incredulous look. "You're standing there in a fur diaper and you're going to give her shit about her bathing habits?"

"All right, that's enough," Trakan says, snapping his fingers at the humans. "Be nice."

"She does not have to be nice," Vaza steps in, protesting. "I like Chail's fire."

Chail just looks back and forth between us, uneasy. After a moment, she lifts a finger and points at Vaza. "If I get to pick, can I be owned by this one?"

Trakan shakes his head. "I don't care. I just need to offload the lot of you."

But I am disturbed by her words. I cross my arms and frown at the one called Chail. "No one is owning you."

Gail tilts her head. "Really? Because it sounds to me like you just bought five humans."

"We wish to have you live with us. You will take a khui and possibly a mate."

The pink one starts to cry and buries her face on her friend's shoulder. "Ohmigod, we're going to be sex slaves," the little golden one with the dark hair whimpers. Even the big one with the pale hair begins to sniff, distressed.

The dirty one just stares at me, and I could swear there is hate in her eyes.

I do not like that they are all upset. This is going very poorly. I turn to Trakan. "We will take them to the village. Get me their fur wraps and boots and I will make sure they are dressed." Surely this cannot be any harder than helping Claire dress Erevair.

But Trakan gives me a puzzled look. "What you see is what you get."

My impatience gets the better of me. I am tired of this fool and have no more use for him, and the weeping of the humans bothers me. For some reason, I feel…guilty, and I do not like it. "Their things. Give me their things and we will take them out of your cave."

"They don't have anything like that." Trakan gives a shake of his head and crosses his arms over his chest. "Sorry."

"Food? Drink? Belongings? Furs?" I am shocked.

Trakan just smirks. "Friend, what part of 'slaves' don't you understand?"

3

ELLY

"You think they're primitives?" Kate asks, tucking a pale strand of hair behind her ear. Worry's written all over her face. Heck, worry is written all over everyone's face, and they look to Gail for answers.

Gail shrugs, tucking her paper gown around her body as if it's a designer dress. "Girl, I don't know what to think anymore."

Me either, and that worries me. Normally you can peg someone by how they react to getting a slave. Sometimes you see that cruel smile spread over someone's face the moment they're given the collar and lead. Sometimes they look at you with disgust, like you're an annoyance they have to put up with. I've had them whistle at me and click their tongues to get me to move, like I'm an animal. Usually within the first five minutes, they show their hand.

But I don't know what to think of these guys, or the fact that one of them left to get us warm clothing.

They're the same race as the two that bought us, but they're different somehow. Their eyes have this weird bluish glow to them, like they're lit from within. They have no tattoos, and they wear what Gail described as a fur diaper and not much else. They wear necklaces with teeth and bone beads, and their long, black hair is smooth and loose, though the younger one has an intricate braid going down the back of his head. Their horns aren't capped with that smooth, shiny metal like the others.

They really do look like primitives, but what are they doing on a spaceship, hanging out with the goons that bought us?

The ones that bought us were easy to peg. The younger treated us like animals, and the older one acted like he wanted nothing to do with us. Despite their scary size, I could handle this. I know what to expect from them.

But these new ones unnerve me. Every time I think I have their behavior figured out, something changes. They bought slaves—humans specifically—so I expect them to treat us like animals. But the elder one with the gray streaks in his hair? He acts like he's in love with Gail at first sight.

So...maybe he's kind. Maybe it's like he said and they bought human slaves because they want mates. Lucky for Gail, I suppose. She's nice, and she's done what she can to protect all of us, so I'm happy for her.

The other one scares me, though. He's a good deal younger than the other one, and taller. His horns arch high above his head, and his face is all hard angles and scowls. And he eyes us like he is expecting something and has been disappointed. I don't know what he wants, but we aren't it.

I'm glad he left a short time ago. I hope he doesn't come back.

I hold my blanket tight around my shoulders and watch as the elder blue guy comes and sits next to Gail. He crouches low beside her and holds out something stringy and dried. "Are you hungry? Would you like to eat?" He speaks English pretty well, though there's a strange cadence to his words.

Her eyes narrow as she watches him, and I know she's trying to figure out his motive. "What is it?"

"Smoked dvisti," he says, though I'm not sure I get the second word right. He offers it to Gail. "Good for travel."

She takes it from him and sniffs it. He beams at her as if this is the best thing he's ever seen, and then looks almost crushed when she breaks it apart and begins to pass it out to the others. We've been fed over the last few days, but there's never enough food to go around for slaves. I shake my head when Gail tries to offer me my portion. I don't think I can eat. My stomach clenches up when I'm nervous and I'll just throw it up.

Considering that I've been nervous ever since we were sold, it's not a good idea to put anything questionable in my empty belly at the moment. I watch as the others eat, ignoring the gnawing feeling in my stomach. I watch Vaza's reaction as Gail nibbles on the smoked meat, but it doesn't look like he's angry, or gleeful at the thought of it making her sick. It doesn't look like he's going to slap it out of her hand. That's good.

"So...you said this was good for travel," Gail comments between bites. "Does that mean we are traveling?" She keeps her tone mild and sweet.

Vaza nods. "We are going to my people's village."

"Is that where your friend went? To your village?"

Vaza shakes his head. "Bek went to get furs from a hunter cave for you. You need warm clothing. Outside there is much snow, and humans are fragile."

I make a small noise in my throat, and Gail glances over at me, even as the others chew, oblivious. She's wondering the same thing. "Do you run into a lot of humans?" Gail asks.

I want her to ask if they have a lot of human slaves. If so, perhaps Vaza is not as benign as he seems. I could expect it out of the meaner, scowling one, for sure. He looks like the type.

"There are many humans in our village," Vaza says. "Many many."

Yes, but are they there by choice? Or were they bought and dragged here to be sex slaves? I'm guessing the latter, and it makes me ill to think about. I thought being someone's zoo pet was bad, but being forced to be someone's sex slave is going to be a thousand times worse.

Gail looks like she has questions, too, but before she can speak up, Summer does. "Caves?" she asks, her nose wrinkling. "Do you guys live in caves?"

Brooke looks ready to cry at the thought.

"Oh no," Vaza says.

Someone sighs with relief.

"We live in huts. Our caves collapsed."

"Oh god," Brooke whispers. "Huts."

"I'm sure they're very nice huts," Gail says, and gives Vaza a saccharine-sweet smile. "And I'm sure we'll be very happy there."

He nods, beaming. "All of our humans are very happy. They have many kits and are content with their mates."

Well, doesn't this just sound amazing. Happy sex slaves busy producing children for their masters. I hug my legs tighter, vowing to fight every step of the way if these bastards even try to touch me under all this dirt. I'm going to make myself so revolting that no one will ever think of it.

"You are very beautiful," Vaza continues, clearly not reading Gail's mood. "It would honor me if you would choose to share my furs."

"Well, aren't you sweet," Gail coos in a voice that sounds completely insincere to me, but Vaza doesn't seem to notice. "I think I need to get settled in before I make any decisions. If it's up to me, that is."

"Of course," Vaza says, giving her another besotted look.

A voice calls out over the intercom. "Bek's on his way back with a sled, Vaza."

Vaza rises to his feet. "Wait here. We will return shortly."

"Oh, I'll be here," Gail says dryly. "Not sure where else I would go."

As Vaza rises to his feet and leaves, tail twitching, I watch him go. Mentally, I play through a dozen scenarios in my head quickly. All of it boils down to one thing—I can stay here and be a sex slave, or I can try to escape. They might kill me for trying, but at this point, I'm not sure it matters.

I'm so tired of someone else owning me.

So before the door slides shut behind Vaza, I get to my feet and hurry after him.

"Elly," Gail hisses. "What are you doing?"

I ignore her. She can stay. Maybe Vaza – or whoever she ends up with - will treat her right. I don't have any such hopes for myself. I'm too unpleasant, too bad-tempered, just like my last master said. The only thing I'm good for is a beating. And these guys are so big that they'll break me. I might die if they catch me escaping, but at least I'll die on my own terms.

I follow a few steps behind Vaza, who is so confident that he never even stops to look behind him and see if he's being followed. He heads down the winding passageways of the ship and then pauses in front of a door hatch. He frowns and smacks a hand, child-like, on the panel of strange buttons. It does nothing, so he smacks it again.

"Quit hitting the keffing door controls," a voice calls out overhead. "I've got it."

A moment later, the door hisses open and Vaza steps out.

And then I see it. For the first time in ten years, I see sunlight.

It's...so beautiful.

I can smell fresh air, too. Not the stale, recycled air of spaceships or space stations. Not the manure stink of a zoo in a private ecology habitat.

The outdoors. The real outdoors.

Intense yearning rushes through me, and I charge after Vaza. It's so close.

I don't even care that the wind whistling into the ship is bitterly cold. I'm just desperately hungry for that daylight, that air. I want to breathe it in and feel human for a short time again. To feel free.

Vaza's down the steps before he realizes I'm coming after him. He turns, frowning, as I reach the top of the steps.

The moment I cross the portal, I'm blasted with arctic, icy air. It's so cold that my lungs hurt. My bare feet, warmer than the metal underneath them, stick to it, and intense pain shoots up my legs. I have so much momentum that I don't realize that the skin on my feet is tearing off until the pain rips through me. I stumble, even as Vaza cries out a warning, and fall off the side of the stairs.

I land a short distance below in a cloud of snow.

Snow.

I sit up, dazed, and scramble to my feet. I can't think properly, but all I know is that I have to get away. There's snow everywhere, though, and my feet are throbbing with pain and the cold. I pant like a wild animal, gasping for breath, and crawl forward. Must get away. Must—

Dear god, is this place nothing but snow? I can't see far for all the flurries in the air, but what I do see is nothing but white and mountains. There's rock, and there's snow...and that's it.

It looks like we've been dropped on this planet's version of Antarctica. Even now, my limbs feel numb and the blood on my feet has crusted over.

I'm going to die. And it's not going to take them catching me and beating me to death. I'm going to die of the elements within minutes. I don't have anything on my body except a thin paper gown. My fingers are numb, and I don't want to breathe anymore because it hurts too much.

But...I can see the sun. No, wait, two suns.

It's so beautiful. I crawl forward, toward those gorgeous suns, and I feel my eyes filling with tears. At least I get to see the sun again before I die.

A strong arm grips my waist, and then I'm plucked off my feet by an impossibly warm body that seems to be a mixture of soft skin and hard bony ridges. "What are you doing?" a harsh voice growls in my ear. "You are going to hurt yourself, fool."

I struggle against his arm, but he's holding me tight. I can't breathe, and I imagine this big arm hitting me, punishing me for escaping. It only makes me fight harder. I'm barely in control of myself as I flail, kicking and scratching. I don't want to be taken back in. I don't want to be put in a cage again.

I don't want to be a slave.

"Stop it," he snarls. "You will hurt yourself. You—"

The shock collar lights up, and then the world disappears in a blast of pain, my brain sheeting white. The last thing I see are the suns, fading out under the agony.

BEK

The female—foolish, foolish female—goes limp in my arms. I scowl down at her, not understanding. Why is she running away? Vaza and I have done nothing unkind. I haul her small body against me, shielding her from the worst of the cold with my body heat. Is there something wrong with her that she would wish to leave so badly? I eye the blood in the snow and her small, filthy feet—now crusted with iced-over blood. She has torn the soles right off of them with her haste.

This one is a fighter. I feel grudging respect for her, even if she is unsuitable as a mate. Far better to have fighters in the group of new humans than the weepers. I hate it when they cry. Claire cried all the time when she was sharing my furs, and it made me feel awful. Like I was being cruel to her simply for disagreeing. I give this female an unhappy shake. "Why do you run away?" I ask. "You are not dressed for this—you will die."

She doesn't answer. Her head lolls in my arms, and for the first time since grabbing her, I realize how still she has gone, so very suddenly. Is she...dead? I am filled with a stark pang of loss that surprises me. I gently grab her delicate chin with my fingers and tilt her face toward mine. Her eyes are rolled back, a line of drool freezing over her cheek even as I watch. But she breathes. Something is wrong, then.

I cradle her against my chest and race back toward the ship. "We need your healer!" I bellow to Trakan's cave-ship, hoping it will let him know. "Hurry!"

Vaza and Trakan both meet me in the entry hall of the cave-ship, and Trakan quickly shuts the door behind me. The other humans huddle against the wall with their thin blankets, looking terrified and upset. The pink one is crying again.

"What is it?" Trakan asks. "What happened?"

"She is unwell!" I hold the fragile, smelly female out to him. "She does not move. We must take her to your healer so she can be cured."

Trakan looks at the female in my arms, and then at me, clearly confused. "I turned her collar on so she couldn't escape."

His words make no sense to me. "Why would a collar stop her from escaping?"

Trakan steps forward. I hold the female out to him, but he does not take her from my arms, simply points at the small band of silvery metal around her neck. "This one's a troublemaker, so they gave her this to stop her from causing problems."

I feel a sick twist in my gut. "What does it do?"

"Well, it sends enough electricity through her body that it stops her in her tracks. I'm guessing she's small enough that it knocked her out."

I do not know what ee-leck-tris-tee is, but the female does not look well. "It is...bad?"

"I guess? I've never worn a collar." He does not look as if he cares, either. "I can imagine it hurts, and it's not my favorite method to discipline, but you use the tools you've got."

Wait...hurts?

He has hurt this female? This small, helpless female who does not weigh even a third of what he does? I growl low in my throat. "You hurt her?"

Trakan looks surprised at my anger. "It's a shock collar. It's not designed to feel good."

I...do not understand this. I do not understand at all. I bare my teeth. Females are precious and meant to be protected, not abused. I look over to Vaza, a warning in my eyes. "Take her."

He steps forward and pulls the female from my arms, cradling her against his chest.

I waste no time; I grab Trakan by the front of his leathers and haul him into the air. I pull him close so I can snarl my words into his face. "You will turn the collar off, now."

"Whoa, Bek, calm down, buddy—"

"Now," I say in a deadly voice. I am shaking with rage. He has hurt a female. Hurt her. All because she was afraid and tried to run. Did he truly think she would go far? I think of the slack look on her small, dirty face, the cold feeling of her thin arms. The blood crusted on her feet.

And this foolish one thought she was such a threat that he hurt her enough that her mind turned off. My own mind is about to go numb with fury. It takes everything I have to control myself.

I am sick that I considered this one a friend.

Trakan babbles on and on about how the collar was not his idea, but I am barely listening. I shake him. "Get it off her. Now."

"You have to put me down first," he cries.

I drop him and look over at the other females, who are clustered in a corner, cringing. "Who else wears a collar?"

"Just Elly," the one called Chail tells me. "We're okay."

I grunt. This is starting to feel very 'not okay' to me. I cross my arms and wait, watching as Trakan moves to the small female's side and pulls the collar off of her. He puts it in his pocket, but I hold my hand out for it.

Like a guilty child, he hunches his shoulders and hands it over to me. I had seen it on the female and thought it was nothing but decoration. Now I know better. I examine it and the delicate parts on the other side. I crush the entire thing in my hand, pleased when it makes a crunching sound, and I drop it to the ground. "Are there other things like this collar?" I ask Trakan coldly. "Tell me now."

"Nothing else."

I look over. "Chail?"

"Nothing else. He's right." There's a bit more confidence in her voice. "Is Elly okay?"

"She needs the healer," I say, and because Trakan is not moving, I glare at him. "Well?"

"Niri?" he asks, tugging on the front of his leathers. "Why?"

"To fix her feet." I gesture at them. "She hurt them stepping outside."

"That's because she stepped on metal in a sub-zero temperature. Her skin froze to it." Trakan shakes his head. "I doubt that—"

"I do not care what you doubt," I tell him. "I want the healer to look at them."

He sighs and rubs a hand down his face. "Kef it. Fine. You're being psycho. I just want you to know that."

I do not know what that is, and I do not care. All I know is that I asked for these females to be brought here, and I will do everything in my power to ensure they are safe.

ELLY

When I wake up, I'm staring back at the ceiling of the medical bay. Oh crap. Not again.

I didn't get away. I close my eyes, steeling myself. My new masters are not going to be pleased. I'm going to be punished.

It was worth it, though. I got to see the sun again. I got to feel fresh air—however cold—on my face. I'd do it again. I'd endure daily beatings if it meant I could go outside on a regular basis. Funny how something so small can become something so important. I never liked to go outside as a kid. Then again, as a kid, I never thought I'd be stolen away by aliens and forced to live in cages for ten years.

"If you're done pretending to be asleep, everyone's waiting on you so they can leave. Us included." The sharp-tongued blue woman speaks somewhere off to my side.

I open my eyes and glance over at her, then sit up, testing things. My head throbs, but that's not unexpected. My feet don't, though, and I see they're wrapped in bandages. I can't feel them at all, and I suppress a bit of panic that they've been frostbitten. I reach down to touch one.

"Leave that alone," the woman snaps. "I gave it a dose of medication to stop infection, but it's going to make it numb for the next few hours. You should be thanking me instead of fiddling with it."

I just look at her blankly. Thanking her? She hasn't been nice to me at all. Her bedside manner definitely needs work.

When I don't respond, she sighs and turns on her wrist communicator. "She's awake. Tell your friends to come and get her out of my medbay."

I hold myself stiffly, remembering to hunch my shoulders so I look thinner and more delicate in case the big, mean one lashes out with his fists. I tilt my head forward, letting my nasty hair hang in my face, and pull my paper gown closer to my body. I wish I had kept my blanket.

The door opens, and the blue guy with tattoos steps inside. Behind him is the big angry one. I can feel myself flinching backward, and I try to scoot back on the table at the force of his displeasure. He storms into the room, heading for where I'm seated, and the urge to flee rushes through me again.

"She should stay off her feet for the next day or two," the woman says, as snappish to him as she is to me. "They're rather torn up."

"I will carry her," the big one says.

Oh no, no, no. I don't want to be carried. I try to get up, to prove that I can walk, but the big blue alien just growls in my direction. Growls. I freeze in place, and he scoops me up into his arms like I'm a damsel in distress instead of a slave.

He's very warm, I notice, even as I do my best not to touch his bare skin. Warm, and his skin feels downy, like suede. It's almost like he's fuzzy, which is double-strange given that he looks frightening as hell.

"Stop moving," he growls at me. "I do not wish to drop you."

I…can't tell if that's a threat. But I know I shouldn't push him more than I've already pushed so far. If my feet are as bad as they sound, there's no running away until they're better. I'm stranded. So I go still, doing my best not to move and bother him.

The big blue alien marches out of the medical bay and down the corridor. He's silent as he walks, and I mentally cringe, waiting for his anger to explode on me. He moves down the halls of the ship, and then, ahead, I see the others waiting. My fellow human slaves are bundled head to toe in a massive amount of furs, only their faces peeping out. The alien called Vaza stands next to them, spear in hand, and it looks strange to see him in a loincloth next to the furry human bundles.

He holds out a big fur blanket to the alien carrying me, and they both pause to wrap me up in the big one's arms. Their hands skate over my body as they do, and I slap their hands away when they get too close to my chest.

"Stop moving," the big one growls again.

I clench my hands. If one of them even so much as grazes a nipple…

But they don't. They only tuck the blankets around me and take care to make sure I'm bundled well. Then Vaza nods at my captor. "Ready when you are, Bek."

So the mean one is Bek. I file that information away, memorizing it. It even sounds unpleasant, just like him.

"We go out now," Vaza says to the others. "It is a short walk to our village. No more than a few hours. Stay close to us and you will not get hurt."

"You're going to beat us if we can't keep up?" someone cries.

Vaza looks shocked. "No, I meant you will not get hurt by wild animals."

"There are wild animals?" Someone else gives a half-scream, and they all cluster closer to Gail.

"Calm down," Gail tells them. "They wouldn't buy a bunch of human slaves just to feed us to bears or something. Like he said, just stay close." She ignores the look of sheer pleasure Vaza gives her and gestures at the others. "This is a lot of change for us. I'm sorry. We'll be quiet and obey now."

Vaza nods uncertainly and looks over at Bek.

"Let us leave this place," my sour captor says. "I do not wish to be here any longer."

Then the doors open, and the brutal wind rips inside again, stealing my breath away. The others squeal at the cold, but the one holding me ignores them. He steps forward and into the sunlight.

And I see the suns again. The sky is a beautiful pale blue, dotted with clouds, and the suns are small and distant, but they're there.

The sight of them makes me so happy.

BEK

It is a mild day of good weather, but the new humans squeal and shiver and whine as if it is the coldest of days in the brutal season. I remind myself that they have no khui to warm them. I remind myself that they have spent their time in the too-warm cave-ship with cowardly Trakan and Cap-tan. That is why they do not like the cold and act as if it is killing them.

But it is still annoying to hear their complaints.

The one in my arms is silent. She is the only one. Even Chail, their leader, has complained to Vaza about the cold. The one in my arms is so quiet that only the constant shivering of her small form tells me she is alive. She, of all of the females, has the right to complain, but she says nothing, keeping her words to herself. Perhaps she is mad about the collar.

She should be. I am still furious. The fire of my anger still burns deep in my belly. It will take many moons for it to leave me. A female should never, ever be harmed. Ever.

That is why I do not care when the big ship leaves again without a goodbye. I watch it go with a cold pit in my stomach and a mixture of anger and gladness in my heart. I do not care if I ever see Trakan or Cap-tan again. I watch the ship rise out of the snow and lift into the sky like no bird flies and then disappear into the skies.

And I am glad for it. The humans are here, and they are mine.

I study the silent one as I walk. The filthy cloud of her mane makes her head look larger than it truly is. Whenever she peeps out from under the fall of it, I see nothing but eyes. She is too thin, I think, her figure more spindly than Farli in her younger years, and so light that I wonder if Erevair weighs more.

She is fierce, though. I remember how she clawed and kicked when I grabbed her. It did not matter that she was hurting—she still attacked. I feel a grudging respect for this small human...even if she smells so terrible my eyes water from the scent of her. She glances up at me, and her expression is blank, but I think she does not like me. I sense it. Sometimes a look flashes in her strange human eyes, as if she would take my knife from my belt and gut me if given the chance.

And I find this...amusing. It is much better than crying.

By the time we make it to the valley, the others are walking slowly, complaining about the cold, the wind, the air, the snow, everything. Vaza is endlessly patient, but I grit my teeth with every new word. I do not have the patience for this. I am a patient hunter...but not when it comes to whining.

So I am relieved when the long shadow of the gorge comes into sight, and the pulley at the lip of it that we use for going up and down.

I am less relieved when it moves and up comes Leezh and her mate, Raahosh. They have their bows slung over their shoulders, and their kits are not with them. Hunting, then. I curse the timing of it, because Leezh has a big mouth. I wanted to go straight to the chief first, to explain myself. Now I will not get that chance.

So be it. I straighten my spine, ready for Leezh's blistering words.

But she only gasps and stares at each human face. Then she turns to me, her eyes wide. "Oh god, Bek. What have you done?"

4

BEK

I will not apologize. I am not sorry for what I have done. I am disappointed I did not resonate to one of the females, but if nothing else, I have given my fellow hunters a chance at happiness.

So when my chief rages at me, I endure it in silence. When his mate just gives me shocked looks of horror, I ignore them. When they ask me, over and over again, "How could you?" I do not change my answer.

I know exactly what I have done.

I have traded shiny bits of metal to a male I will never see again in exchange for mates for my friends. I have brought new people into our tribe. I can see no wrong in this, even if my methods were not what Shorshie and Vektal approve of. How else are we to get mates for the other hunters?

It is easy for Vektal to sit and judge me with his pretty mate at his side, his kits at his feet. He has everything he has ever wanted. He has not had to stare down seasons of loneliness, wondering if he will ever have a mate, a family. If he will ever be complete.

"You are not listening to me," Vektal snarls, a hand-span away from my face. "I tell you how disappointed I am and you gaze at me with that blank expression on your face."

"Vektal, honey," Shorshie says in a low voice. "Calm down." She gets to her feet and hands him his smallest daughter, Vekka. "Hold the baby."

He scowls at his mate but takes his little daughter from her, clearly not done raging. The moment she is put in his arms, she sucks her thumb, gazing at him with big, worried eyes. He sighs and hugs her close, patting her back. "Calm. I am calm."

Shorshie shoots me an angry look, but her voice is calm. "I just don't understand what you're thinking, Bek. You can't steal people and bring them here."

"I did not steal them," I tell her. "Trakan did."

"He stole them for you. That's just as bad! Why would he do such a thing?"

"We became friends," I tell her, though now the words feel sour on my tongue. I think of him using the collar on the small, dirty female and feel shame. If he does not know that hurting females is wrong, how can I trust his other decisions? "And the females will be happy here."

"You don't know that," Shorshie exclaims, and she is so loud that her daughter jumps. With a frustrated sigh, she takes little Vekka back from Vektal and hugs her close, trying to calm herself down. "You don't know that," she repeats in a lower, calmer voice. "They might have families at home. Jobs. Things they care about. Or hey, here's a thought—they might not want to spend the rest of their lives on an ice planet making blue babies."

"But you are happy here. The others are happy here."

"Because we fell in love," she hisses, stroking her daughter's hair. "That's different."

"They will fall in love as well," I tell her. "Once they receive their khuis, they will take mates and be happy. It will be as it should."

She stares at me, as if my words shock her. "You're delusional. These things take time. You bought slaves and brought them here, Bek. How can you not understand how wrong that is?" She shakes her head again and then pinches her brow. "This is not the same as when Maddie and Lila were found. I can't believe you don't realize that."

"I have broken no rules," I tell them.

"Why would we have rules against buying slaves? This is a peaceful place!" Shorshie hisses again, then collects herself, pressing a kiss to her daughter's cheek. "Maybe you'd better see Papa again, Vekka."

"I think perhaps her mother needs to keep holding her," Vektal says. "My temper is fine."

Shorshie shoots him an angry look as well and then turns back to me, still holding her daughter close. "You haven't broken a rule, only because it's not something anyone ever thought would come up. That'd be like us having rules for not murdering, or stealing children. It is shit you do not do." She punctuates each word with angry enunciation, patting her infant daughter's back as she does. "I just...I just can't believe you, Bek. I really can't."

"My mate and I will discuss punishment," Vektal tells me in a sour voice. His other daughter, Talie, rushes up to his legs and holds out a piece of leather to show to him. He absently picks her up, pulling her against his side, and she begins to braid his hair with the leather. "I do not know what we can do that will make you understand the severity of your actions, but do not think you will get away with this."

I nod slowly, expecting this. "Of course, my chief. I am prepared for whatever you decide."

Shorshie does not look pleased, though. Perhaps because the last few times that Vektal disciplined tribesmates, it ended up not being as harsh as it could have been. She tilts her head and studies me. "I have to ask. You got five women, right?"

"Yes."

"And did you resonate to any of them?"

I see where she is going with this, and I scowl. "Not yet."

"Good." The vehemence in her tone surprises me. Shorshie has always been pleasant. "I hope you don't resonate at all, because that's the worst punishment I can imagine for you—to know that you stole women and then you have to give them to everyone else."

My jaw clenches. I say nothing, because she is not wrong. If none of the females here resonate to me—ever—it will be the worst possible thing I can endure. She knows how badly I want this, and her words cut like a knife. I have been burying my disappointment so far, but it is difficult to see the females standing in front of me and know my khui wants none of them. Once again, I worry I will be left with nothing while the others around me celebrate their happiness.

Shorshie gives me a tight smile, as if she knows her words have found their mark. "If you'll excuse me, I have some human women to welcome to Croatoan." And she marches away with Vekka in her arms, her back straight.

I watch her go and then turn to Vektal. Even he seems surprised at his mate's vicious words, a rueful smile on his face. "She is protective of her people, my mate."

I grunt.

"I would ask that you stay away from the females until they are settled in. You being around them will upset the other humans, because they will think that we approve of you stealing females."

He is not wrong...but I do not want to stay away, either. How can I resonate to one if I am hiding away on the hunting trails? Even though it pains me to think it, I also feel protective of the small, filthy one. She has been abused under my watch, and I should be there to guard her and ensure she remains safe until she resonates to a male that will protect her. "They will need khuis very soon," I tell him. "They do not handle the cold well."

"I know this," he grits out, his voice dangerous even as his daughter plaits his hair from her perch in his arms, oblivious to her father's mood. "It will be soon."

"I am a good hunter. You will need me with you."

"We will take all of the unmated males with us on the sa-kohtsk hunt. We have no choice, thanks to you. The more I hide them away, the more tension it will create. Better to see who they resonate to and handle it as it happens." He shakes his head.

"Stop moving, Papa," Talie tells him in a piping voice, putting a small hand to his cheek. "I am making your hair pretty."

"Apologies, little one." He goes still and just glares at me while his daughter begins her braiding again.

And I am filled with a keen, bitter yearning at the sight. That Vektal, who is such a fierce hunter, has a little daughter to hold close, a daughter that is the same deep blue as him, has the same eyes and her mother's strange curly hair. I want daughters. I want sons. I want a mate.

I want a family. I am so tired of being alone.

"I know you are angry," I tell him, clenching my fists at my side so I do not speak loud enough to scare Talie. "But there is nothing I want more than what you have. I want a mate and kits at my own hearth. I—"

"I understand," Vektal interrupts.

He does not. He will never understand. "You do not," I say fiercely. "You mated the first human female you saw. And then Pashov mated, and Zennek, and Raahosh, and everyone else. And then more females came, and again, I watched others get their heart's desire and received nothing for myself. So until you know what it is like to watch female after female mate to other hunters while you are alone, you do not understand."

Vektal just shakes his head at me, pity in his eyes. "And it might be happening all over again."

The sick clench in my gut tells me he is right. Once again, others will get their mates while I stand to the side, watching.

Alone.

ELLY

"I know it's cold," Georgie says briskly, setting her daughter down on the stone floor. "But I promise you it gets better over time. And when you get your cootie, you won't even notice the cold." She pauses, thinking. "Much."

I take the thick fur she hands me and wrap it tight around my shivering body. It doesn't feel as if it's making much of a difference, so I move back closer to the roaring fire.

The other four women and I are in a stone hut in the strange little village that these people live in. When I'd heard the word 'hut' I'd expected something extremely primitive and made with mud. This isn't quite that, but it's not exactly a Ritz, either. The walls are made of stone, the ceiling something like a teepee to let the smoke from the fire out. The interior's bigger than I imagined, about the size of an Earth bedroom, and the floor is stone. There's a nook with a toilet, a long bar along the back wall that serves as a counter, and beds of furs on the floors. It actually isn't all that bad. Considering I've lived in cages for the last several years, I like it. The air is fresh, and I can stand completely upright, so I'm happy.

The others aren't quite as happy as me. There are still some tears and lots of worry, no matter how much Georgie and the other females reassure us that we're safe and no one's going to own us. I can tell Gail is skeptical, especially because every woman that comes in has a blue baby in her arms.

It's not something you accept right away.

One of the women says her name is Stacy, and she sets up a little tripod over our fire and begins to add chopped vegetables and meat to a hanging pouch. A waterskin is passed around, and everyone drinks thirstily—except me, because I don't know these people. I don't trust them not to drug the water. I'll wait and see how the others react to it. As Stacy fixes the stew, Georgie keeps handing us furs, and another woman by the name of Kira sits with us and tells us what she can about this place.

The story of how these humans got here is awfully familiar. The stories of the small green aliens that stole them from their beds, waking up to find your world is gone and you're now someone's property—it's like what happened to me. Except these women were adults when they were taken, and I was thirteen. These women were left behind on this planet instead of sent off to the slave markets. We weren't quite so lucky.

Kira's calm voice is soothing as Georgie laces a tunic over Summer's dainty form. She tells us about being rescued by the sa-khui—the big blue guys—and how their ancestors were stranded here many, many generations ago. They have lived here happily despite the cold, and continue to do so despite an offer to return to their homeworld. The humans elected to stay with them, happy with their mates and families.

"What about home?" Kate asks. "Can we go home?"

"The only ship capable of going back to Earth is the one you came here on," Kira explains, her small daughter sitting in her lap. The child watches us with big eyes, as quiet and thoughtful as her mother. "I'm afraid that we're hunter-gatherers here, with very little technology like you're used to in the past. No television, no phones, no internet, not even running water."

"Oh lord," Gail says, shaking her head. "And you guys are happy here?"

Kira shrugs. "We weren't given much of a choice in the beginning, just like you, but we came to love it here. The sa-khui are wonderful people." She thinks for a moment and then adds, "I know it's hard to believe, considering Bek's actions, but we're all very upset at him."

"Don't forget Vaza," Georgie calls out, handing Summer a boot. "He's not getting off scot-free either."

"But the ship," Kate persists, leaning forward. "The ship can come back and get us, right? Take us back to Earth? What if we offer to pay them?"

"Earth isn't considered an 'allowed' planet," Kira says gently. "No one will go there. Even if the ship came to get you, they'd just turn you over to the nearest alien authority. That's one reason why none of us wanted to leave—we couldn't guarantee we'd ever see our families again. Humans are forbidden because our planet is considered too primitive by most alien cultures."

"But, but, but," Kate protests, and gestures at the stone walls of the hut. "What do you call this?"

Kira gives her a faint, sad smile. "Generations of survivors doing their best with what they've got."

"I want to go home," Brooke says. "Can't you make them understand that? We don't want to be here."

"Unless Bek has a deal with *The Tranquil Lady* that I don't know about, I doubt they're coming back. I'm afraid you're going to be with us."

Summer sniffs, and Brooke starts weeping into Gail's fur-covered shoulder. The other women look awkward, and Stacy grabs a stack of small bowls and starts ladling food out. "You girls need to eat something. You'll feel better with a full stomach."

Bowls are passed around, and Stacy hands one to me. I shrink back and turn my head away, declining it. I'm hungry, but I've been served bad things from a smiling face before. I need to trust before I can relax enough to eat.

She looks surprised at my refusal and glances over at Georgie.

Georgie shrugs. "Give her time."

"Well, we should probably tell you guys everything, because I don't want anyone to be surprised," Kira continues. She smooths her daughter's hair away from her small face and smiles down at her.

"Your daughter's cute," Gail says, smiling at the little girl. "Her daddy's clearly one of the blue guys."

Kira nods. "My mate is Aehako, and we resonated."

"Is that why your eyes are glowing blue?" Gail asks. "Because of this 'resonance' thing?"

"Yes and no. The blue is because of the khui and all of the things that it does for us." The expression on Kira's face is serious as she continues. "You might not like what I have to say about it, but you deserve to know everything." She glances at Georgie and Stacy and then continues. "Every living thing on this planet has what is called a 'khui.' It's a symbiont that enables you to survive..."

HOURS LATER, most of the women have left. Kira and her small daughter have stayed behind, camping out with us, I think to give a sense of comfort. Of trust. She seems nice, but I cannot unlock my worries enough to be friendly to her. To anyone.

The others sleep peacefully, someone snoring gently. The hut's warm and comfortable enough, though there's a chill in the rock floor that won't go away no matter how many layers of fur I pile on top of me. The bedding is nice, too. If these people are sincere, this won't be so bad...

But I can't trust yet. I can't trust that I won't wake up and find myself in a small, horrible cage again, surrounded by wild animals and prodded with sticks because I'm a strange 'creature' to an alien culture.

I can't sleep, either. I'm too busy thinking about everything we've been told.

This planet has no spring, no summer. There are two seasons—a bitter and a brutal. One where the snow is mild, and one where the snow is gut-wrenchingly awful and the cold is horrendous…and that's the one that's coming up.

Everyone here has a parasite that's both good and bad. It's what makes their eyes glow and keeps their bodies healthy, and we're going to get one in a few days. I don't like the thought, but no one asked me.

I like what the parasite does even less. Kira called it a khui, though the others jokingly called it a cootie. And it seems that the cootie also controls reproduction. That means if it decides it likes someone on this planet, I don't get a say in things. It'll vibrate in my chest—resonance—and my 'mate' will vibrate, too. It's also going to make us incredibly horny until we give in and have sex, after which I'll have a baby.

The thought terrifies me. Even though Georgie and the others stress that we're not slaves here, if I resonate I'll have a big brutal alien man who will have a say in everything I do, because I'm carrying his baby. It'll be just like having another owner, but this one is for sure going to want sex. I swallow hard, queasy at the thought, and sit up. The need to escape is hitting me hot and heavy once more, but I know there's nowhere to go. It's an ice planet where there's no warm weather, ever. Leaving without the proper gear would be a death sentence, and I like living. I keep hoping that someday I'm going to have a real home, where I can live on my own terms. Where I can see the sun every day. Where no one will ever put me in a cage or collar me like I'm a dog.

I just have to survive until then.

It occurs to me as I lie in bed that there must be stars here on this planet, though, and I'm hit with an intense wave of longing. I want to see the stars.

Badly.

I crawl to my newly-healed feet, still wearing the borrowed leather clothing and boots I was given. Whatever foot-wraps they gave me on the ship must have had some serious healing power, because they feel new and don't hurt when I walk. I'll take it.

I feel the chill in the air the moment I leave my bed, but I won't be gone long. I just want to gaze up at the stars and see them. I know it'll make me feel better. So I pick my way through the scatter of beds on the floor. Kira and her little daughter are snuggled up close by the hanging flap they call a door, and she yawns and glances up at me. "Don't go too far," she murmurs. "It's too cold at night."

I give a little nod to acknowledge her words, stepping under the flap and outdoors.

The cold hits like a punch in the face, but I'm ready for it. I brace myself, shivering, and walk a few crunching steps out over the snow-scattered cobblestones. There's someone sitting across the way near a fire, and he nods at me but doesn't get up. Of course we have guards watching us. For all the lip service about us being free, we're strangers to them and they don't trust us yet. As long as he leaves me alone, though, I don't care. I just tilt my head back and gaze up.

God, the stars here are beautiful.

The night sky is a mere sliver thanks to the high walls of the canyon the small city's located in, but what I can see is a deep, lovely shade of midnight that looks like it's been sprinkled with glitter, there are so many stars. Some of them are clustered so tight together that they look like reddish clumps, and there are green waving lines in the sky that must be an aurora of some kind. I've never seen anything so beautiful.

It makes me so happy that I feel tears welling up. Lovely, lovely stars.

"It's nice, isn't it?" a soft voice behind me says, and I jerk around, stiff until I see Gail's small form. She comes to my side, blankets wrapped around her, and gazes up at the sky while standing next to me. "Never seen any stars like that in my life. Wasn't sure I'd ever see them again after what we've been through."

There's a knot in my throat that won't go away, because I know what she means. In some of my darkest hours, stuck in a small, stinking cage, I wondered if I'd ever breathe fresh air or see daylight again. The stars feel like a present, just for us.

"You okay?" she asks softly. "I noticed you didn't eat."

I shrug, keeping my head tilted back so I can keep gazing up at the beautiful night sky. Maybe after I get my parasite, I'll sleep under the stars every night. I think I'd like that. Never be caged in again, if these people are to be believed.

"I know what you're thinking," Gail says. "Me too. Seems too good to be true that we're gonna be free and just part of their little happy village." She's like me, she doesn't trust. It doesn't matter that they greet us with smiles on their faces. Actions are what matter. "But I think," she continues, "I *hope* that they're good people. They seem happy."

They do. And they're generous. I don't even mind the whole no-warm-months thing, not really. But the thought of having a cootie implanted in me that chooses my mate? That scares me. What if he's...awful? What if he uses his fists to get his point across? I rub my breastbone, thinking of what it'll feel like if I resonate.

"Yeah, I worry about that, too," Gail says. "Under all that dirt you love, I know you're young. Me, I'm fifty. I'm not having any more kids. Had one son and that's it."

I look over at her in surprise, because I didn't know she'd left family behind on Earth.

Her smile is soft, her eyes shiny. "Nah. He's not waiting on me. Died when he was sixteen in a car accident and broke my heart into a million pieces. Me and his daddy separated after that." She looks up at the stars. "I'd love more babies, though. Love their voices, their little hands, their sheer joy. The thing that troubles me is that I went through menopause last year. So I'm hoping these aliens are forgiving of something like that, because if they expect me to have a baby for them, it's gonna be bad." She pauses. "I'm worried what will happen when they find out."

Me too.

She sighs heavily and looks up at the stars again. "I suppose I'm just borrowing trouble, though. Maybe there's room for an old lady that can't have more kids. Just like maybe there's room for a girl who keeps herself covered in dirt so no one will look twice at her."

Busted.

Gail knows my tricks, I guess. Not that it matters, because she's not going to call me out in front of the others. She respects a defense mechanism. I can't worry about it. There are so many things to worry about, I'll never sleep again if I focus on all of them. So I just look up at the stars again. They'll be back tomorrow, and so will the sun. I suppose there is always that to look forward to.

With one last look up at the stars, I head back inside.

5

BEK

For two long days, the humans are kept locked away in their quarters. They need time to adjust, Shorshie tells everyone. Time to relax and not be scared of this new world they have been dropped on.

It is making the unmated hunters crazy. They find ways to wander past the hut where the females are, curious to get a glimpse of them, to see if their khuis respond. So far, no one has resonated, and in my small, mean heart, I am glad the others are as frustrated as I am. Of course, they do not resonate because they have not seen the females face to face. I have spoken to all of them and still my khui is silent.

Of course, since Vaza and I are the only ones to have seen the human females, it means we are constantly harassed with questions. I ignore them, because what can I say? It will not matter what the human looks like if there is resonance. Young Taushen could resonate to the filthy, angry little scrap of a female and resonance will not care. Quiet Warrek might resonate to the female that Vaza adores, and Harrec might resonate to the one with pink hair and the constant weeping, and they will drive each other mad. Resonance does not care. It only wants them to mate and create kits. It knows better than we do.

Vaza gives them enough descriptions to whet their appetites when I do not, though. He talks of beautiful, delicate Chail with her dark skin and tight cap of gray curls. He speaks of the pink-haired one with the big teats, and the golden one with the silky black mane. He talks of the tall, strong one with the pale cloud of hair, and both Taushen and Harrec seem interested in that one. And he speaks of the smelly one that is too thin, who is nothing but eyes and dirt.

No one is interested in that one. I cannot blame them—she is unappealing as a mate, with no strength to her limbs, no rounded softness like the other human females. She has no smiles or sweet voice, and she stinks. Whoever resonates to her will have a tough trail ahead of him, and I do not envy that male.

Well...I envy him a little.

Vaza is talking about Chail's dark eyes and her pretty smile around the fire this morning when Raahosh storms back into the village a short time after leaving. That gets my attention and I straighten by the fire, dropping the spear I am sharpening. Raahosh heads directly for the chief's hut and disappears inside.

I know what this means. I fight down the surge of excitement in my chest and glance over at Vaza and Harrec. "I think Raahosh has found a sa-kohtsk."

The other males leap to their feet, excitement in their eyes. "If that is so, then we must gather all of the unmated hunters,"

Harrec exclaims, no trace of his normal sly laughter in his manner. "And this means we get to meet the human females."

I nod curtly. "Go find Taushen and Warrek. I will speak with Vektal and see what I can find out."

I head through the village, making a line for the chief's hut. The females are out and about, but as I walk past, the human mates of my friends and fellow hunters ignore me. They are all angry at me—even Claire wept and ranted at me for what I have done and barred me from her fire until she has forgiven me. I feel a pang of grief at losing her friendship, but she does not understand. No one does except the other unmated males who have felt nothing but despair.

I am a hero in their eyes.

I reach the chief's hut as he emerges, and he has his spear and hunting weapons strapped across his back. Raahosh follows close behind him, his scarred face tight with anger as he gazes at me. My chief nods in my direction. "It is time. A sa-kohtsk has been spotted in the valley."

So close? That is excellent—it means the fragile humans will not have to go far. "Harrec is getting Taushen and Warrek. We will be ready."

Vektal nods. "Leezh will be coming with us. She will guard the human females." He fixes his gaze on me. "And you are to stay away from them."

Of course. It will not matter if I walk next to the females or ahead of them—resonance will decide.

And perhaps today, resonance will decide in my favor.

ELLY

It's funny; out of all the humans on the ice planet—Not-Hoth as I've overheard someone call it—Liz seems like the one that belongs the most. Kira and Georgie and a few others that I've met seem like nice, normal young moms.

Liz seems like a Valkyrie.

She marches at our side, wearing light furs compared to our swaddles, and wears her snowshoes like she was born to them. There's a bow strapped to her back, knives at her belt, and her long blonde hair is drawn back into a tight, no-nonsense braid. She barks commands at us as we waddle like ducklings behind her. Someone mentioned that Liz has two young children, but she doesn't strike me as all that motherly to us. Her mate is a big scarred brute that scares me every time I see him, so maybe she's learned to be fierce to keep up with him. She's got a sharp tongue and she's not afraid to use it.

Like right now. "Come on, Pinkie Pie. I know you can pick your feet up higher than that," she calls to Brooke, who's lagging behind for at least the fifth time in the last hour. "Don't make me come back there and get you."

"I'm tired," Brooke yells back at her. "I'm not an Amazon like you! I can't do this!"

Liz only grins and jogs back to her side. "The sooner we get there, the sooner you get warm. You want warm, don't you?"

I'm pretty sure Brooke flips her the bird. I'm also pretty sure Liz sees it and laughs. Her bright mood makes me relax a little, though.

It's been a weird morning. The moment we were told that it was the day to go hunting and get our cooties, it's been non-stop racing around. I'm exhausted from the walk, and we haven't even made it to the hunt yet. I managed to steal a few mouthfuls of food when Liz brought out rations and then ate a big chunk of it, figuring that she wouldn't poison herself, but it isn't enough to give me much energy. Every step feels like exhaustion, and the snowshoes I'm wearing make it difficult to lift my feet. We're all struggling, though, except for tall Kate, who must be in better shape than the rest of us.

Half of the hunting party ranges ahead of our straggling group. Liz's scarred, scary husband and another pair of hunters bring up the rear, but the majority are far ahead. They watch us closely, and there's far too much interest in their eyes when they look at us. It makes me feel uneasy to catch them glancing back, because I know these are probably the ones that want mates.

They're checking us out for potential.

The thought makes me huddle deeper into my furs, pulling them tighter around my face, until the only thing exposed are my eyes and my dirty mop of hair. I'm extra glad for my itchy, dirty filth today because they look at me, and then quickly move on to gaze at Kate, or Brooke, or Summer. That suits me just fine. I don't want to be anyone's mate. I want to be my own person. I want to be free.

It's cold as hell, the wind ripping at our layers of clothing, but the suns are high in the sky. I can't say that they're bright—I suspect this planet's farther away from its suns than Earth was to its, but it makes me happy to see the blue sky and breathe in the fresh air, no matter how frigid.

One of the hunters far up ahead stops in his tracks and waves his spear in the air, then makes a gesture. Liz raises a hand in acknowledgment and then jogs to the front of our small line.

"Okay, ladies. The hunters have spotted our critter. This thing's called a sa-kohtsk and it looks like a furry Macy's Thanksgiving Day float with toothpick legs. I don't want you to freak out if you see it, because we're going to have to get up close and personal with it. They don't eat people, so don't worry about that. And they move slow. The hunters are going to bring it down, and then we'll move in so you can get your cootie. Any questions?"

"Yeah, can we go home yet?" Brooke asks.

"Very funny, Pinkie Pie. You can go home once you've gotten your cootie." Liz grins. "You guys are lucky this thing is so close. Sometimes we've had to walk for days to find a sa-kohtsk."

This is close? I feel like we've been walking for hours, my fingers numb from cold, and judging from the cranky sounds the other humans make, I'm not the only one who feels it. But Liz isn't panting with exertion, or even slowing down, so I press on.

She leads us toward a cluster of spindly trees that look more like hairy toothpicks than actual trees. They're a soft pink color, and when I reach out to rest my hand on one, I notice it's not exactly sturdy—and that my hand comes away sticky. Ugh. I wipe it on my furs and shoot a furtive glance at the others to see if anyone noticed.

That's when I hear it.

Thud.

Thud.

Thudthud.

My insides seem to shake with every thump, and for a moment, I wonder if someone's throwing boulders off of one of the distant cliffs. The ground itself feels as if it's quivering.

"Look sharp, ladies," Liz calls out, and points off into the distance.

I glance over and suck in a breath.

There, lumbering in the snow, is the biggest damn creature I've ever seen. It's hideous and terrifying all at once. The mouth is enormous, and the four glowing eyes set in the head remind me of a spider. There's fur all over the damn thing, and Liz is right—the legs are toothpick-like and long. As each foot steps to the ground, the earth shakes again. Jesus. I feel a sense of panic at the sight of it, stepping backward.

"Lord almighty," Gail breathes.

"What is that thing?" Kate asks.

"It's the sa-kohtsk, and what our boys are hunting today. Stick close to me," Liz says, and she looks unafraid. "We've got the best seats in the house for the show."

We huddle closer to her, as if Liz can somehow protect us if that thing veers in our direction.

It's slow moving, the sa-kohtsk, and after watching it for a few steps, I'm fascinated by its lumbering gait. It almost moves as if it's slogging through water, which I find fascinating. Maybe its big body is too heavy for it to move faster, but it doesn't seem to be in a hurry, even when it gives a low bellow of anger and I see the blue bodies racing alongside the legs of the thing. They look tiny next to it, even though I know they're just as overgrown in their own way.

"Taushen's already right on it," Liz murmurs. "This shouldn't take too long, then."

I watch the hunters move around the much larger animal, and find myself fascinated. They're graceful on their feet, racing next to it and darting in and out between its legs as if playing the world's scariest game of chicken. As they move, the creature veers in one direction, only to have another hunter race up on the creature's side and begin to swipe at the legs, herding it in the other direction. It makes a low moaning noise and continues to lumber forward, churning endless amounts of snow in its wake. The creature heads toward our copse of trees, but Liz doesn't move an inch.

"Um," Summer says. "Should we move?"

"Nah," Liz tells her, never taking her gaze off the hunt. "They won't let it get near us."

She's right. In the next moment, the hunters are racing along-side the treeline and jabbing spears at the enormous legs, herding it carefully away from us. I notice out of my peripheral vision that Gail and the others are taking a few steps back, but I don't move. I'm too fascinated by the hunt. They're so graceful and fast. I'm filled with envy at how free they look, how strong. I want to be like that.

As they race past, the hunters get close enough that I can make out individuals instead of just blue blurs. The one in the lead is unfamiliar to me, his hair long and flowing behind him as he yips and slashes at the big creature's legs. A tall one races on the far side of him, and he's got a wide smile of delight on his face even as he dodges one of the enormous feet. They look like they're having fun. One of the other men skirts wide, moving close to us, and shoots a scowl in our direction, as if he disap-proves of how close we are.

I'm not surprised to see that it's Bek. That one always seems to be frowning. But Liz doesn't pay any attention to him, and so I don't move, either. If anything, I stand taller and straighter. We're not doing anything wrong.

A few more people race past, and the creature stumbles, starting to lose its footing with the constant harassment from the hunters.

"Might wanna turn away if you don't like blood," Liz says, arms crossed as she watches. "This next part's not gonna be pretty."

I don't turn away, though. I want to see what happens.

In the next moment, before anyone can ask, one of the hunters makes a flying leap, knife in hand, and grabs on to one of the creature's tall, spindly legs. He stabs at the bend of it, and then blood arcs through the air, steaming and bright red.

I suck in a breath at the sight, surprised at the brutality of it. The big sa-kohtsk stumbles, falling forward onto one knee, and then the hunters swarm over it. More blood spatters the snow as they attack it with knives and spears, and I watch, horrified and entranced at the same time, as Bek moves to the creature's head and stabs his spear into one glowing eye, and is promptly soaked with blood.

Someone behind me gags.

"Yeah, it's not pretty," Liz says mildly. "But it gets the job done. Once everyone stops puking, we're moving in, so grab your stuff and be ready to move. We have to get in there before the blood freezes because the cooties don't live long in this environment."

We wait while Gail—strong, capable Gail, of all people—finishes puking in the snow, and then Liz herds us forward. The hunters still move over the carcass of the thing, calling out to each other and laughing, the high of the hunt still coursing through their veins. I know how they feel, I think. It's like I've been given a shot of adrenaline just from watching them. I step carefully through the blood-covered snow, keeping close to the others even as I stare in fascination at the big carcass of the creature. It's so huge. Wow. There was nothing this big in the zoo I was kept in for so long, and my memories of elephants on Earth don't compare to this thing in the slightest. The closest thing I can think of is like a humpback whale on stilts. The mental image makes me smile, though it falters when several of the hunters slit the chest open and more blood pours out. Eesh. So much blood.

Gail begins to gag again, and we pause, waiting for her. I notice I'm standing close to one of the long legs, and I feel a twinge of sadness that such a magnificent, albeit weird-looking, creature has to die so I can live. "I'm sorry," I whisper quietly to it, not that it can hear me.

"Grab one side, and I'll get the other," one of the hunters says. "Let us make this quick."

As I watch, the tall, lanky hunter moves next to the quick one, and they grab at the thing's rib cage.

Meanwhile, Bek moves toward our group, a thunderous frown on his hard face. "What is taking so long? Come forward."

"Oh, hold your horses," Liz tells him. "We've got a puker."

"Then—"

Anything else he says is lost as the two hunters pull the ribs apart with a thunderous crack. As they do, the creature's body jerks. I scramble away a few feet, trying to get away from the legs because I don't want to be kicked.

Bek snarls and tackles me.

BEK

She is running away.

Again.

The small, dirty human with the feisty mind is trying to run again? Anger and frustration explode through me as she backs away a few feet, her big eyes wide with fear. I remember Leezh was full of fear when given her khui, and others fought as well. This one is a runner.

Instinct takes over and I grab her, knocking her to the ground. I keep my grip loose, careful not to hurt her.

She makes a noise then, a little scream of horror. Kicking at me, she scrambles out of my grip. Her foot connects with my jaw, and I nearly bite my tongue off with the force of her blow. I am determined, though; she will not get away.

Mine.

I growl and snag her ankle even as she scuttles backward, and she makes another awful little crying sound. She's thrashing in earnest now, her eyes wild like a trapped dvisti. I know this one. I know she will not stop flailing until she is free, no matter how much she might hurt herself.

So I hold on tighter and use my arm to pin both of hers against her sides. She's thrashing angrily, her feet kicking and hammering against my thighs. If she were any bigger, she would do real damage, I realize with rueful admiration. As it is, the only thing that hurts is my jaw.

"Bek, what the fuck?" Leezh calls out.

"She was running," I grit out, carrying my squirming burden toward Taushen and Harrec, who are carefully pulling the heart out of the sa-kohtsk's chest. "Give this one a khui first."

"You're scaring her," the human called Chail tells me. "She doesn't like to be touched!"

I ignore her. This one cannot keep running. Not now, when she needs her khui. I grab her chin with my free hand and do my best to block out her whimpers, though I feel like a monster even as I do. "I will hold her still. Harrec, cut her, and Taushen, give her a khui. Do so quickly."

They nod and get to work. Harrec leans in with his knife, giving me a reluctant look before speaking to the small human that even now squirms in my arms as if she will fight until her dying breath. "Forgive me, little one."

She jerks, making more whimpering sounds when his knife cuts into the side of her neck. It is a ceremonial cut, and not deep, but I hate that it must be done, and she is so full of fear. This one is so brave compared to her sisters. I press my chin down atop her head. "Shhh. It will be over soon," I murmur to her, low enough that it is only for her ears. "I will not let them hurt you."

Her squirming slows, her breathing still raspy and quick, but I am pleased when Taushen pulls out a long, gleaming khui. It is a strong one. Good. And I am even more pleased when she goes limp in my arms as it disappears into the wound, the khui's work beginning.

I should set her down on the snow, let her rest. Instead, I cradle her close, protective even as she is unconscious. When she wakes up, I will apologize for my harsh handling of her. Until then, I will guard her close. I tuck her small body against my chest.

Immediately, Chail runs up to me and smacks my arm. "What the fuck? I told you she doesn't like to be touched and you're manhandling her! Is this how we're all going to be treated?"

I bare my fangs at her. "If you try to run away, yes."

Vaza steps in front of Chail. "Bek, be reasonable—"

I growl at him. He takes the female's side because he wants her in his furs. He is obvious. "I am doing what is best for the female, Vaza, and you know it. If she runs away, we risk losing the khuis, and then we will have to hunt down another."

He nods slowly. "Then at least put her down so the other humans will not be so frightened."

Frightened? Because I am holding the small, dirty one? I gaze down at the female and realize I am clutching her against my chest. Her filthy hair brushes against my face, and the stink of her is eye-wateringly bad. But...the urge to protect her is near overwhelming. She is so fearful that she is not careful with herself, so I must watch out for her. Surely they see that.

But Leezh looks over at her husband and then gestures at me. Raahosh comes forward and puts his arms out. "I will take the girl to Leezh, and she will watch over her. You are frightening the others."

What he says makes sense. It should not matter if I hold her as long as I can stand guard. However, the thought of giving her over to him feels like a punch to the gut. I do not know why I feel so attached. My chest is silent. It is not resonance. What is it, then?

Reluctantly, I hand her over, hating the way her head lolls as he carries her to Leezh. He should be supporting her neck. He should cover her legs with a warm fur so she does not get cold. He should—

"Are you going to stand there all afternoon like a stone, or can we give the other humans their khuis?" Harrec asks, voice dry with amusement. "I can try to go around you, but you are much larger than them."

I turn and give him a scowl and then stalk away.

ONE BY ONE, the humans are given their khuis. They immediately fall unconscious, slipping to the snow in the deep slumber that their bodies need to adjust to the change. They were braver than I expected, however. Even the pink-maned one did not cry as the knife was brought to her throat and the small cut made.

We settle blankets around them, make them comfortable under the trees, and wait. Raahosh builds a fire for his mate, and we guard the large carcass from predators that might come into the area. Sa-kohtsk are not good eating, but so much meat will draw something for certain, and we must be ready.

I find myself standing by Taushen, scanning the valley for the loping slink of snow-cats or the wings of a scouting scythe-beak. He stands next to me, spear in hand, and then glances over. "Do you...feel any different?"

"Eh?" I look over at him.

"Resonance." He puts a fist over his heart. "Did you?"

I shake my head. "Nothing. You?"

"Nothing." The disappointment is obvious on his face. "I thought for sure it would happen for me." Taushen sighs heavily, his shoulders slumped. "I remember when the first humans arrived. It seemed that at the sight of them, the others resonated right away. Vektal resonated to Shorshie before she even had her khui. Yet I look at these females and I feel no different."

I grunt. He speaks aloud the same worries I have had. "My sister has an idea as to why no one has resonated to them yet." She told me about it last night, and I have been thinking about it ever since.

"Oh? Maylak?" Taushen looks interested. "What does she say?"

I nod. "She thinks that so many resonances happened right away because there were so few females in our tribe, and even fewer kits. We were dying out. With the humans here and new kits born every season, there is less urgency. She thinks that resonance will take longer to happen."

His mouth turns down in a frown. "I hope she is wrong."

I hope she is, too. It seems unfair to think that because others got their mates, I will have nothing. To see human females in front of us and still not resonate, it seems cruel.

I have had a pleasure-mate in the past. I suppose I could take one again. The thought fills me with disgust, though. My mating with Claire burned hot for the first turn of the moon and then quickly changed to ash. It left me hollow inside.

This time, I want the real thing.

KATE IS the first of the humans to awaken, her eyes shining bright blue. She sits up in surprise, then moves to the fire, and then stares at her hands in even more surprise. "I'm not as cold as before."

"Winner, winner, chicken dinner," Leezh says happily. "Don't worry, you'll like the cootie." She pats the snow on the ground. "Come sit next to me while we wait for the others to wake up."

Kate does, and I watch her and her strange, pale mane. She is tall and strong. Healthy. Surely she will be someone's mate? But I feel nothing for her, and my khui remains silent. If I am to resonate, it is not to her. I eye the other hunters and notice they are all watching her with avid stares, hunger in their eyes.

No one steps forward. Kate yawns and smiles at Leezh. "Have anything to eat?"

Rations are shared, and we go back to pacing, watching the humans and waiting for them to rouse. The one with the golden skin—Suh-mer—is the next to awaken. And again, I feel nothing. My chest is silent. So are the others.

I can feel the despair in the air as Chail awakens and no one resonates to her. Vaza is delighted, though, and quickly moves to her side with a gift of his waterskin and some smoked meat. Buh-Brukh—the pink one—is the fourth to awaken, and I have to admit to myself I am glad when my chest remains quiet. She is a weeper.

Only the small, dirty one—Ell-ee—still sleeps. I rub my chest, gazing over at the small pile of furs where she slumbers. Some do not take to their khui. Sometimes the body is not well enough to handle it, and I think of her fragile bones and how thin she is. How hollow her eyes are. What if she does not awaken? The thought is unbearable. She is strong inside, a fighter. It is not fair that her outside should be so delicate.

As she continues to sleep, I find myself watching her instead of the others gathered near the fire. Why does she not wake? Has no one bothered to check on her? What if she is ill? What if she needs the healer even now?

I bite back the growl in my throat and surge forward, storming over to her furs. I must see for myself that she breathes.

"Bek?" Harrec calls. "What is it?"

I ignore him and pull the blankets back, revealing Ell-ee's face.

Her eyes open, a bright, brilliant blue, and she scowls up at me, jerking the blankets out of my hand and wrapping them tightly around her body again. She is...pretending to sleep because she does not want to talk.

I chuckle and rub my chest. Clever little thing. How often have I wished I could walk away from an annoying conversation by the fire? She is wise to feign sleep. I should apologize to her for grabbing her earlier, if she does not like touching. I should let her know that it is not safe to run away.

I should tell her a great many things, but they all fly out of my head, thoughts scattering like startled dirt-beaks, because my khui begins to sing when she narrows her blue eyes at me and frowns, her hand over her own heart.

6

ELLY

I knew it.

I knew the moment we were told that our cooties might pick a mate that I'd be trapped, forced to belong to someone again. It doesn't matter that the humans here spout that we'll be free and smile to reassure us—you always end up forced to rely on someone in the end.

I was praying it wouldn't be the mean one, though.

I've just woken up, my thoughts scattered and confused. I can hear voices and the scent of smoke that tells me there's a fire nearby, so I remain where I am, feigning sleep while I sort through my emotions. I'm not as bone-deep cold any longer, which is strange but nice. There's still a bit of a nip to the weather, but under the blankets, I hardly notice it. I wonder if my skin is as feverishly warm as the blue aliens feel. I mentally examine my body, looking for other physical changes when I realize...I'm wet between my thighs.

Just thinking about it makes my pulse throb right at my groin.

Under the blankets, I furtively cup my sex, worried. I've never felt need before, not like this. As I was barely a teenager when stolen, I missed out on everything that normal girls do—dating, flirting with boys, prom, the works. I spent most of those years in a cage and was paraded as a pet the rest of the time. If I had ever showed any inkling of sexual need, my owners would have either tried to breed me to another slave to produce more pets or taken the task upon themselves. So I made sure never to seem like anything other than a fragile dirt-farm.

I've never even so much as touched myself properly, though I've thought about it a few times. But there's never been enough privacy, and the need hasn't been there. I've been just fine without touching myself.

The need's there now, with a vengeance.

I don't know what to do. I don't know how to get rid of it. All I know is that I ache deep inside, and my nipples are hard, and I feel...restless. Unsettled. Full of hunger for something I can't describe.

At least, I can't describe it until someone walks up to my bed and yanks the furs back, exposing me to the world.

I shouldn't be surprised to see that it's the mean one—Bek. My hands fly to my chest, to cover my fluttering heart as I gasp in shock. He gazes down at me with those slitted, hard eyes, his mouth a firm line that shows no gentleness. I realize a moment later that my heart's not fluttering. It's my brand-new cootie, and it's resonating.

To him.

To the one that scares me more than all of the others. The one that tackled me the moment I stepped near the fallen creature.

The one that put his hands all over me and sent me into a blind panic. I vaguely remember kicking his jaw, but I also remember that he'd pinned me against him and held my face so the others could cut me, and I'd loathed every moment of that.

I also remember his voice, soft and soothing, as if trying to comfort me. It doesn't fit with my memories, though, so I discard that and stare up at him accusingly.

"You," he murmurs, dropping the blanket to crouch near me. He looks thoughtful, and then a slow, hungry smile spreads over his face as he watches me. His hand presses to his heart, and I can hear his cootie humming in time with mine, the din of them drowning my senses.

I watch him, uncertain what he's going to do now. Throw me onto the snow and force himself on me? It doesn't matter that the others are nearby—I don't know these people and what they're capable of. I do know that they don't give two shits about nudity, because I've seen a lot of blue beefcake—and human women, too—in the few days that we've been at their village.

"My mate. I should have known," he says in a low voice, his eyes bright. "Such a little fighter."

I don't feel like fighting right now. I want to burrow back under the blankets and hide away from the world. I want this all to be a bad dream. Instead, I think of his big hands as he'd grabbed me earlier, and I'm filled with sheer, unrelenting fear. This one is going to touch me, and it's going to hurt. How can it not? He handled me so roughly just a short time ago, and I stretch one filthy arm out, looking for bruises, because I'm still hurting. Sure enough, there are fingermarks on my arm where he'd gripped me. I look down at them and at him accusingly.

He sees them, and the look on his face is nothing short of horror. And that...surprises me. I was expecting a 'I told you not to run' or a 'That's what happens when you misbehave' or a 'Get used to it, bitch' sort of comment. I certainly don't expect him to go pale, his throat working as if he's having a hard time swallowing.

"Was that from me?" he asks.

I just glare at him. What, does he think I magically bruise myself while I'm sleeping?

Bek scrubs a hand over his face, the hard lines of his mouth pulling down even more. "I am...ashamed. Forgive me." He extends a hand out, reaching for my arm. "Let me see it."

I shrink back, my stomach churning at the thought of letting him touch me. Touches aren't good. They lead to other things. I've seen that happen too many times before.

"What are you doing?" someone calls out, and I realize it's Liz.

Bek turns toward her, and as he does, I reach out and snatch my blankets back. He looks back at me, surprise on his face, and our eyes meet. For a moment, it's like I'm sinking into his bright blue gaze. I'm trapped there, and my cootie hums and sings in my chest even louder, making my nipples tingle and ache against the thick leather of my tunic. He seems to hold his breath, and the air around us feels electric.

And god, I am ridiculously wet, my pulse pounding so hard it feels as if my cootie's making it sing, too.

Liz's boots crunch in the snow as she approaches, and she frowns at Bek, who's still kneeling far too close to me. "You're not supposed to..." Her voice dies away, and her eyes widen. "Oh, you've gotta be fucking kidding me. You two are resonating?" She shoots a horrified look back and forth from me to Bek and then back to me again.

Bek straightens, his body tall and strong and delicious and alarming all at the same time. His tail flicks as he stands, annoyed. "She is my mate. Our khuis have chosen."

I might be wrong, but it sounds like there's pride in his voice. If so, I suspect that not even my layer of dirt is going to protect me from his attentions. For some reason, the thought makes me squeeze my thighs tighter together.

Liz arches an eyebrow at him and then looks down at me. "Yeah, well, she doesn't look thrilled."

"She will be," he says, all confidence.

"That so?" She cocks her head at me. "Elly, are you thrilled?"

I don't look over at Bek. I just give a small shake of my head, clinging to my blanket.

"Think you'll be thrilled in the next five minutes?"

Again, I shake my head.

"Next day?"

Still no.

"Okay then, I'm stepping in." She steps fearlessly between us, as if Bek isn't enormous and bulky and scary, and puts a hand on his chest. "You go away. I'm sitting with Elly and guarding her until we get back to the village."

Bek scowls. "She is my mate. We are resonating. You—"

"You need to talk to the chief, Mr. Rule Breaker. As long as Elly's scared of you, you're not breathing the same air as her. Understand?" She puts her hands on her hips. "Or did I miss the part where you grabbed her and flung her around and forced her to get her khui?"

His face goes bleak for a moment and then stiffens into something like a scowl. "She must have a khui."

"Yeah, well, there are ways to do it and ways not to do it. You and Raahosh must have been comparing notes or something."

Somewhere near the fire, it sounds like Raahosh snorts.

I should speak up. Say something. Take charge of my own life. Tell Liz what I want. Tell Bek to go away and leave me alone. But the words die in my throat and I can't get anything to come out.

The other humans move away from the fire, and I notice that Summer, Kate, Brooke and Gail have bright blue glowing eyes now. Mine must be glowing, too, though my vision looks the same. To a one they all frown at Bek as they walk past and come sit in the snow next to me. They sit close, but not too close that I panic. It's a show of solidarity and sisterhood from women I've never spoken to, and the knot in my throat seems to get suddenly huge.

Someday, I'm going to tell them thank you. For now, I just press my fist over my breast and wish my cootie would stop humming so mercilessly.

BEK

Of course it is Ell-ee who is to be mine, I muse as we head back to the village. My heart is full of joy. I do not even mind that the other humans walk with Ell-ee at the front of the group and I walk at the back with no company except Raahosh. That is fine —they will not be able to separate us forever. Resonance will not allow it.

The other hunters sneak me envious looks; no one has resonated but myself and Ell-ee. They will have to wait for resonance to choose them at a later date, if it will choose at all.

Resonance.

Just thinking about it makes my khui begin a slow, steady song. It has finally happened, and my female...she is perfect.

Well, she smells bad enough that my eyes water being near her, and she will not speak, but I know Ell-ee is the mate I have been waiting for. Even when she is at her most afraid, she does not cry. She is brave. Determined. Clever.

Mine. The thought fills me with pride. Over time, perhaps she will learn to enjoy washing. For now, I am more concerned that she is so frightened of me. Can she not speak, ever? Or does she choose not to? Would one of the other humans know? I focus my gaze on the one called Chail, who has taken a motherly role with the other females. Even now, she rubs an arm over the pink one's shoulders, encouraging her.

Chail would know if Ell-ee can speak.

I jog forward, ignoring Raahosh's muttered curse. He does not pursue me when I move to stand next to Chail and walk next to her. They want me to keep away from my mate. I ignore the anger that burns in my gut at the thought and focus on Chail.

She notices I am walking at her side and gives me a side glance. When I do not leave, she frowns. "Can I help you with something?"

Her words are polite, but it is strange; her tone does not indicate she wishes to help at all. "I have questions for you."

"You assume I want to talk to your blue ass."

"Not my ass," I correct her. "You can talk to my face."

Chail gives herself a little shake, her brows scrunching down. "Are you fucking with me?"

"No. I wish to ask you questions about Ell-ee."

"And if I don't feel like talking to you?"

It is my turn to frown. Why will she not speak with me? "I only wish to learn more about my mate. You know her better than I do."

"Yeah, I do," Chail says slowly, shrugging her fur wraps tighter around her small body. "And I'm sure that she's not happy to be your mate."

I look up ahead, at the stiff-backed figure of the one who is my mate. She seems so fragile and alone, even though Leezh and Harrec flank her. "Why does she not speak?"

"Maybe she doesn't want to talk to you."

I turn to her. "So she talks to you?" I am relieved. If this is true, it means I can win over her affections. In time, she will speak to me.

But Chail purses her lips. After a moment, she shakes her head slowly. "No, she doesn't talk to me. She doesn't talk to anyone. But I know she can speak." She glances up at me. "I've heard her say things in her nightmares. And they weren't good nightmares, just FYI."

The urge to protect my mate rushes through me, and I clench my fist on my spear, resisting the need to rush to her side and pull her close to me, to comfort her for past memories. "So she chooses not to talk." She is strong-willed, my mate. I feel fierce pride at that, even if I am frustrated by her silence. "Did something happen that makes her afraid to speak?"

"You'll have to ask her."

I will. Perhaps she will even answer me. But not today. I look down at Chail again. "Can you tell me anything else about her?"

She does not seem happy at my questions. "Why do you want to know?"

Did I not make that obvious? "I wish to learn more about my mate. I want to know what pleases her. I want to make her happy."

Chail gives a little snort. "What would make her happy is not resonating to you, but I guess that's off the table. Is it true that it's unbreakable? Resonance?"

I confirm this with a nod. "Many were initially displeased with their mates before they realized their khui had truly chosen the right person. Resonance always wins."

Chail hums over this. "And what happens if you try to ignore it? If you fight it?"

Humans always ask this. Always, the answer is the same. "Resonance chooses. It is foolish to fight it."

"Yeah, well, I'm not asking if it's smart. I'm asking what happens."

"The need to mate grows greater with every day. It will make you weak and miserable until you accept it." I rub my chest, where even now, my khui is singing low, waiting for another glimpse of its chosen mate. "But resonance is what everyone hopes for. It brings mates together and brings new life to the tribe. It is a good thing. As her mate, I will take care of Ell-ee and see that she is happy."

Chail ignores my proud words. "So basically this cootie thing is going to force her to have your babies." She shoots a skeptical look at me. "And here I thought you guys said we weren't slaves."

I scowl. "You belong to no one. Why would you think that?"

"The cootie's making her be your wife. How is that her choice?" She glares up at me. "How do I know the moment our backs are turned you're not going to grab her and rape her? Hold her down until she 'accepts' your mating?" She wiggles her fingers in the air.

I watch them, confused. "What is that?"

"What is what?"

"This?" I wiggle my fingers at her. "Is it like this?" I show her my middle finger, a gesture that Leezh has made a lot of use of in the past few seasons.

"Been flipped off a few times, have you?" Chail has a strange look on her expressive face. "Those are air quotes, and don't change the subject. Are you going to rape her?"

I am offended she would think such a thing. Ell-ee is mine to cherish, mine to protect. I would never harm her or force myself upon her. "It angers me that you even ask that."

"Put yourself in my place. You think how safe you'd feel if you were in my position? I've seen you with her."

And that makes me silent, because I did grab her near the sa-kohtsk when she tried to run. I think of the marks on her thin, dirty arm and feel shame. And I think of the collar that Trakan put on her, and my gut twists. Chail is right not to trust. "I do not wish to hurt her. I wish to..." I choke on the words, overcome all at once by the joy and frustration and emotion of having a mate after all this time. "I wish to...love her. I want nothing more than her happiness."

"Well, then you would be the first," Chail says drily. "Let me tell you what I know about Elly, then. I know that her last master used to keep her collared like a dog and made her crawl around on all fours, naked, just to humiliate her. He didn't think humans were smart or feeling, so he left a shock collar on her all the time. I know that she doesn't trust anyone, even me. I know she won't eat if she doesn't trust the food given to her. I know she has nightmares. I know she's terrified of being touched, and when she's scared, she retreats to small, tight spaces to hide. That tells me she's been abused in the past, quite a bit."

Each word she speaks feels like a knife. She is telling me such horrors...about my mate. I cannot bear it. "Stop," I say hoarsely. "These cannot be."

"Why not? You think everyone's all happy and Brady Bunch-like your tribe? You bought slaves, my friend. You know who buys slaves from a slave market? Depraved, sick sons of bitches that don't have an ounce of compassion. To them, we're not people. We're currency."

Some of her words make no sense to me, but there is a vehemence in her tone that tells me everything. "I only asked for females to be brought to our tribe so our unmated hunters could have families."

"You. Bought. Slaves. Don't think anyone's going to forget that anytime soon." Chail's voice is sharp. "I've been a slave for eighteen months now, and let me tell you, it's hell. I've been beaten, whipped, slapped, fed garbage, sold to strangers, and treated like an animal. And that was only eighteen months. I feel like I've aged eighteen years in the time I've been captured." She gives a slow shake of her head. "Elly's never said, but I can tell in her eyes—that girl's been in this system for years. Maybe even longer. Who knows what it's done to her."

I cannot think. All I can do is stare at the small, straight back of my female. My dirty, silent female.

My female who hates to be touched.

"I will not touch her unless she asks me to," I tell Chail. "You have my word."

"Honey," she says with a small, bitter little laugh. "I don't trust your word for shit."

"A SHUNNING," Vektal announces when we return to the village.

I was surprised when the entire village met us as we returned from the sa-kohtsk hunt. A celebration is being held in the long-house, as the humans call it, and I can smell food roasting, and Farli has already started decorating her mate with her painted symbols. The humans are embraced and welcomed into the tribe.

All except for Ell-ee, of course, who does not want to be touched.

News of our resonance trickles through the tribe, and my chief strides forward, his mate at his side. Everyone waits, watching us. And that is when he pronounces his decision.

A decision I am not sure I understand.

"Eh?" A shunning? This is something I have not heard. I look at Vektal's mate, the still-angry-at-me Shorshie. Her arms are crossed over her chest, and the look on her face is resolute. This is her idea, then. "What is that?"

"It's clear that you don't have the tribe's best interests at heart," Shorshie begins.

Do not have the tribe's best interests at heart? Did I not ask for enough humans for all of the unmated hunters? How is that selfish? I scowl in her direction.

She continues, her mate nodding approval. "So because you decide you don't need the tribe's laws," Shorshie continues, "We have decided that we don't need you. You're officially shunned from the tribe. No one will acknowledge that you are here. You are not welcome in the long-house. You're not welcome in any of the tribe's huts or at any fire. You will be ignored by any and everyone in the tribe as if you don't exist."

This is...the most foolish thing I have ever heard. Ignored? Ridiculous. "I am a hunter. You will need me to hunt."

"We will make do without you," Vektal says. "You may get your things from the hut you share with the other hunters, but then you are shunned. I am sorry to have to do this, but I hope you will learn your lesson."

This shunning seems a silly punishment. "And my mate?"

"She's not shunned," Shorshie says in sweet voice. "She is more than welcome to stay unless she wants to go with you."

I look over at Ell-ee, hope in my eyes. I know it is early and we have only just resonated, but perhaps...

But no. She shrinks back, averting her gaze, and ignores me. Very well. She needs more time. I have waited many, many seasons for my mate. I can wait a few days longer. I devour the sight of her, unable to look away. "Who will take care of her?" My voice is hoarse with need. "May I hunt for her?"

"If you like," Vektal says. "But if she wants you to leave her alone, you should."

"How long is this 'shunning' to last?" I ask, annoyed.

"Until you realize what it is you've done," Shorshie says firmly. "And judging from your reaction, we've got a long way to go."

"Your shunning officially begins now," Vektal says, crossing his arms over his chest. "As of this moment, you do not exist to this tribe."

I snort. Somewhere off to one side, Harrec guffaws.

Vektal shoots him an angry look and then gestures to the others. "Come. Let us celebrate the new members of our tribe in the long-house."

I scan the faces of my tribesmates as they turn and leave. A few of the hunters—my friends—seem confused, but they follow the chief reluctantly. There is hurt and betrayal on Claire's expressive face as she holds little Erevair in her arms and turns to leave. The hurt on her face wounds me. She acts as if I have done something wrong. Does she not see I had no choice? "Claire," I begin.

She ignores me, walking a little closer to her mate.

"Ell-ee," I call out, hoping she will turn.

She does not.

I am well and truly shunned...and I do not know what to think.

7

ELLY

"He's still hanging around the damn village," Tiffany says, shaking her head as she braids long strands of leather into a thick woven mat. "I don't think he grasps the concept of 'shunning.'"

"Oh, I think he does. He just doesn't care. Bek's stubborn like that." Claire works on the other end of the mat, pleating her strands.

We're all inside the long-house on this day, the weather nice and sunny. The leather roof of the building is rolled back so the potted plants Tiffany nurtures here can get some sunlight. A few of the pregnant women are talking to Brooke and Kate by the fire, and off to one side, Gail is making trail rations into cakes and letting little Lukti, Erevair, and Zalene help her. I can hear their laughter, and it makes me smile. Gail is so happy to have children around. She loves them and loves helping out.

Claire picks up another strand to weave into the rug and shrugs her shoulders. "You know Bek. I'm pretty sure part of the reason is to remind us that he's there, and part of it is because he doesn't know what to do with himself. And well, let's be honest—part of it is Elly."

From the corner of the room where I'm standing with a waterskin, I can feel my cheeks heating. It doesn't matter how many times Bek comes up in the conversation on a daily basis, my name is linked with his. It's a small tribe, Georgie has told me when she caught me looking embarrassed. They gossip. And since we've resonated, we're everyone's favorite topic. New people would be fodder for months as it is. New people that resonated in such a fascinating way? I'm screwed if I think no one's going to be talking about it.

And Claire and Tiffany are both nice. They're calm, easy-going personalities—unlike the bossy Liz or the boisterous Maddie or endlessly chatting Josie—and they're fine with my silences. I fill my waterskin with warm water from the spring and go back to watering the little fruit trees. It's one of the few tasks I can do around here, and I'm happy to do it. The roots and soil are covered with thick dvisti hides, uncovered to be watered, and then covered again to protect them. I've watched Tiffany grab the pots and move them into the sunlight as the suns travel overhead and the shadows grow long, so I do that, too. It's a full-time job just taking care of these trees, but there are little buds of fruit growing on them and everyone's quite excited to have them to eat soon.

"You'll make Elly uncomfortable," Tiffany chides her with an apologetic glance over at me. "She knows he's coming around to see her. No reason to bring it up and make things awkward."

I give her a faint smile of thanks and move away to water the trees on the far side of the long-house, closer to Gail and the children. I don't know if I want to hear more of the conversation, just because Claire was good friends with Bek and likes to talk about him. Hearing his name makes me feel funny, like I can't decide if I want to run away screaming or if I want to squeeze in next to her so I can hear every gory detail. I know that Claire's his ex-girlfriend. I feel weird about that, too, even though it's clear that Claire's wildly in love with her sweet husband, Ereven.

It's been a week since the sa-kohtsk hunt, and everyone's still adjusting and finding their place. Kate and Liz connected well, and now Liz and her mate Raahosh are showing Kate how to hunt, because she wants to learn. Brooke tends to linger by the fire to hang out with whoever is there, and spends her time braiding hair and trimming ends. It seems that Brooke was a hairdresser back on Earth and wants to save everyone's hair here. Most of the women are happy to let her beautify them, and I notice that she chats a lot with Stacy and Nora, who take over a lot of the cooking duties and are thus around the fire a lot as well. Gail watches many of the children and helps Ariana with classes and teaching. Josie and Lila are teaching Summer how to sew, and their laughter can be heard in the small village often.

Everyone seems to be finding their spot except for me. Of course, that's not unexpected. I've set myself apart from the others. I still haven't bathed. I still haven't spoken, though I've wanted to a few times. I still wake up in the middle of the night in a cold sweat.

I'm just...waiting for the other shoe to drop, I guess. I'm waiting for something to happen that will turn this place from a wintry paradise into another nightmare. Until I truly feel safe, I'm going to keep on as I am. If that means I don't have the friends that the other girls do or blend in like they do...it's just safer. I won't get hurt that way, not if I'm expecting bad things to happen. It's when you let your guard down that the awful comes.

"Look everyone, it's Miss Elly. Wave to Elly," Gail says cheerfully, and gives me a happy wave.

The three children seated in front of her wave also, their hands dirty with fat and seed mixture.

"We're making trail rations," Gail says. "It's important for everyone to know how to do it, isn't that right?"

Lukti, a quiet little boy with blue skin and a head full of tight curls, smiles at Gail and holds a cake out to her. "I made this one for you."

"Oh, I'm not hungry." She holds her hands up, smiling, and then nods at me. "But I bet Miss Elly's hungry. Why don't you ask her if she wants it?"

Lukti looks over at me shyly, and then scoots closer to Gail. "She doesn't talk," he says, worried.

"Elly smells bad," Zalene declares, patting her cakes laid out in front of her. "She's stinky."

The children giggle, and Gail just shakes her head. "Miss Elly can wash when she wants to, because she's a grown-up. She has her reasons, and it's not for us to be mean and say she's stinky. Apologize, Miss Zalene."

"I think Elly is nice," Erevair declares, and gets to his feet and runs over toward me. He holds out a sticky, mangled-looking patty of something that's supposed to be food. "I made this for you."

I take it awkwardly. My stomach growls, because I'm still not getting enough food. In the last week, huts have been set up for the humans, and I'm currently rooming with Gail. We've been given piles of supplies and some food for our hut, but I can't bring myself to eat it. I don't know who it's come from. I don't know if someone's slipped something awful into it. And I know that these people are nice and kind and won't do that, but I still can't bring myself to take a bite out of it.

So I only eat when there's a community stew, which means I get about one real meal a day. I'm ravenous all the time, and even the sight of this well-handled little cake is making my stomach churn with hunger and anxiety. I don't know what to do. I want to eat it...but my brain wars with my worries.

I hold it, frozen in place.

As if she can read my mind, Gail leans forward and takes another one of Erevair's cakes and nibbles on it. "Mmm, these are so good, Mr. Erevair! You have a gift, little man."

He beams at her, all pride, and I shove the cake into my mouth, chewing furiously. I'm so hungry.

Zalene looks at me funny. "Elly's weird," she declares a moment later.

"Is not," Erevair says, beaming at me. "She's Bek's mate, and that makes her great."

I choke on the mouthful of food.

"Bek's my friend," Erevair tells the others happily as he returns to his seat. "When he comes back to the tribe, he's going to show me how to hunt."

"Is he now," Gail murmurs, shooting me an apologetic look. "And Miss Zalene, we don't tell people that they're weird. It's not nice."

Zalene shrugs her little shoulders. "Mama says that Bek isn't nice. She says he's a *tête de noeud*. Mama says that means dickhead in her language."

A horrified laugh chokes out of Gail, though she tries to smother it. I press a hand to my mouth, silently laughing even as I chew. Bek is a dickhead? It fits. I decide I like Zalene's mama, even if her child is a little talky.

"Is Vaza your mate, Gail? Did you resonate to him?" Lukti asks, all innocence.

"Resonance is gross," Zalene declares. "My mama says that resonance makes you want to put your tongue in the other person's mouth. Yuck!"

"You don't need resonance to do that," Erevair tells them. "I saw Vaza do that to Gail yesterday."

Oh really, now? I know he's been coming around our hut, always with gifts in hand, but I hadn't seen that. I give Gail a surprised look.

Gail clears her throat. "You don't need resonance to kiss someone, no. And Miss Gail is far too old to resonate, because resonance wants babies, and I can't have any more. But if Mr. Vaza wants to have a friend, I might be that friend." She gives me a coy little look and grins. "But he's gonna have to work for it." She primly adjusts the hem of her tunic, looking pleased with herself.

So Gail's encouraging Vaza's flirtations? I shouldn't be surprised. Vaza is like a puppy around Gail, eager to please and willing to do whatever it takes to make her happy. If she mentions that her pillow is flat, he makes her a new one. If she mentions a specific fur is soft, he brings her three more for her bed. He's constantly stopping by to talk to her, and I know she keeps him at arm's length, but I also know she isn't chasing him away.

I wonder what that means for me if they get together. Of course, it's stupid to think about that. Everyone assumes that I'm going to end up with Bek because we're resonating. The thought makes me uncomfortable and restless, and I finish watering the plants, then head out of the long-house. I need to be alone to clear my thoughts, catch my breath. The others are happy to be around company all day long, but it gets to be too much for me quickly, and I need fresh air. I could spend all day and all night just gazing up at the sky, out in the open, and so I take every opportunity I can to soak it in.

You never know when it'll be taken away from you again.

So I walk through the village, giving the friendly people that say hello to me a polite nod or two, but I don't go over to meet Georgie, or to greet Megan or Kira, who stand talking nearby with Kemli and Sevvah. I keep my head down, my hair in front of my face, and head for the outskirts of the village. I grab a woven basket as I pause near my hut at the edge of town and take it with me so I look like I'm going to be busy. I can go collect a few dirt-beak nests for fire fuel, get away for a bit, and then return when I'm settled mentally.

A short distance away, the canyon forks in a few directions, and there is a marked path that leads toward the little cove where the dirt-beaks make their nests. It's one of my favorite places to go and get away, but before I can turn onto the path, I see another person—a sa-khui male—heading into the village even as I leave it. I duck my head, avoiding eye contact.

My cootie starts to hum, and I know who it is, even without looking. I feel that full-body flush move over me, feel my nipples get tight and my female parts get slippery and hot. God.

Why does he have to show up now, when I'm alone? I hurry down the path toward the dirt-beaks, hoping that he won't notice me. That he's busy or bringing in food and he'll go straight into the village and I won't have to worry that he's going to follow.

I know that won't happen, though. And I feel a weird little flutter in my belly because I'm so unsure of what to think.

In the last week since Bek has been 'shunned' by the tribe, he's still hanging around. He lurks on the edges of the village and always seems to be close by. It's like he doesn't know—or doesn't care—that he's being shunned. No one talks to him, but he continues on about his business like it's no big deal. In the mornings, he makes a fire on the outskirts of the village and sharpens his weapons there. He hunts and brings back fresh meat for the tribe, and if no one thanks him for it, he doesn't seem to mind. I'm not sure where he sleeps, but he's always close by, it seems.

I shouldn't notice, and I shouldn't care, but I do. It's the cootie, I think. It's got me all turned around. I'm restless at night, and when I do dream, they're disturbing and erotic and I wake up feeling more achy and needy than ever.

Behind me, I hear footsteps on the snow-scattered cobblestones. My breathing quickens, and I feel the flutter in my belly go wild again. I want to not care that he's following me, but I'm acutely aware of every single step he makes. I clutch my basket tighter and speed up. Should I go back to the village? Hide inside my hut for a few hours? The indecision torments me. I know it should be a simple decision to make, but with the cootie humming in my breast, I can't seem to do it.

"Ell-ee," Bek says, voice low and husky as he moves to my side. "You should not be out here alone."

Oh, I see. He's trying to make it easy for me to dislike him today? I can do that. I shoot him an irritated look and step carefully away from him, making sure that my strides put distance between us.

He keeps pace with me, though, and if I go any faster, I'll be running, and that's just ridiculous. I slow my steps, holding my basket tight and keeping my gaze directly on the ground in front of me. I can see his legs if I peek over out of the corner of my eye, and the butt of his spear as it thumps the ground. He holds a dead, spiky-looking animal in his other hand, no doubt another kill for the tribal stewpot. I wish he'd go away and hand it off so he can leave me alone.

I think.

Because even as the words circle through my mind, I realize I might be lying to myself. I'm scared of Bek, but at the same time, I find myself grudgingly fascinated by him and by our connection. I think of when he'd held me against him at the sa-kohtsk hunt. I should be mad about him clenching my jaw and the bruise he'd left on my arm, but all I can think about is how he'd tucked his chin into my filthy hair and whispered to me to calm me. The look of pride and joy on his face as we resonated, as if he was glad—glad! —to be the husband of the dirty mute girl.

Sometimes I think he sees me underneath all this grime. That I can't hide from him. The idea is both terrifying and exciting.

"I wish you would speak to me." He continues to walk at my side, keeping his pace with mine. If I slow my steps to a crawl, his slow, too. "Not because I feel you owe me an explanation," he goes on. "I simply wish to know that you are well. That you are doing all right. That the others are treating you kindly." He pauses. "And...I admit that I wish to hear your voice."

My skin prickles with awareness at his words, an odd form of pleasure. I don't speak, though. I don't know if I can, yet.

"I know you are not comfortable enough to talk to me. That you worry what our resonance means. But I am a patient hunter, my Ell-ee. I can wait for you to come to me. Resonance might make my cock ache, but I can ignore it. I want you to want me as much as I want you."

Well, that'll never happen. I give a little snort, my only concession that I'm hearing his words.

"You can think what you like," Bek says, and there's amusement in his voice that adds a rich tone. I like it. "But I know you still feel fear. I know you do not sleep well at night. I know you do not eat much. But you are my mate, even if we have not yet touched, and I will do whatever I can to make you happy. If you do not like the food, I will bring new foods for you. If you are cold at night, I will bring you furs. If you are lonely or sad, I want to comfort you."

Nice words. But I never believe words. They're far too easy to speak and they don't mean anything.

"I dream about you at night," he murmurs, and my skin prickles again. I've been dreaming about him, too, and the flashes of my dreams that float through my thoughts make my cootie purr even louder. I can hear his purring, too. "When I first saw you," he continues, "I thought you were strange but so very brave. It was clear you were scared, but you never cried, and you did your best to escape. And I thought to myself, this one is strong. She does not cry and weep like the others. She knows there is risk in escape, but she takes it anyhow. She is brave. And I thought that if I should have a mate, she should be strong like you. Instead, my khui has given you to me." There is a ragged little catch in his throat, as if he's emotional, and a sympathetic knot forms in my own throat. "So even though this will take time, I want you to know that you have as much as you need. I am here for you, and I vow to you that I will never touch you in anger, or in menace. I will never force you. When we come together, it will be because you want me, too."

More words. Sweet words, but still as empty and cold as the air around me.

There's a long pause between us as we walk, and then Bek grunts. "I wish you would acknowledge that you have heard me, at least."

I shoot him the bird.

A moment after I do, I regret it. I'm impulsive despite my fear, and I worry it's going to cause me to get hurt again. *Will you ever learn, Elly? Jesus.* I keep my shoulders stiff, mentally cringing, waiting for him to strike me.

But I only hear a startled laugh. "I will take that response, Ell-ee. Thank you."

And I smile to myself under my cloud of dirty hair.

Bek seems to run out of words after this. We make it to the dirt-beak nesting grounds, a honeycomb of cliffs that are wall to wall with dung-nests, like swallows back on Earth. I expect him to leave now that he's said his piece, but he unstraps his weapons from his waist and sets his spear and his kill down and then proceeds to help me fill my basket with the precious empty nests. They're easy enough to collect, but it's kind of nice to have quiet company, even if my khui does thrum and sing in my chest the entire time.

When my basket is full, I try to pick it up, but Bek makes a surly noise in his throat that makes me skitter backward in fear. He sighs and hefts the basket under one arm, as easy as if it were full of feathers. "I would never hurt you," he growls.

More words. Just more words.

We walk back to the village in silence, and he drops the basket in front of my hut and then pauses for a long, long time. I stare at the toes of my boots, wondering if he's watching me, and if he is, what he's thinking. But eventually, he turns and leaves. I glance up to watch him go, but he doesn't turn back. I grab the basket and decide to take it to the long-house.

As I do, I notice little Erevair standing in the doorway of the long-house, watching. He smiles at me like he has a secret.

Maybe he does. I don't suppose I did a great job of shunning Bek after all.

BEK

I watch my mate go back to the village without me at her side, and I feel...frustration. Anger. Sorrow. Longing.

This 'shunning' is nothing but stupidity. I can lurk around the village as much as I want, and all they do is pretend not to see me there. They will take my food I bring, my fuel for their fires, but they will not speak to me? It is childish nonsense, a game to them.

Meanwhile, my mate lives with another and I must see her only when she slips away from the others.

Patience, I remind myself. This is good for Ell-ee even if it makes my spirit hurt. In the days that I have left the village and the humans have been settling in, I have seen the hunted look fade from Ell-ee's eyes. Her shoulders are a little straighter when she walks. She is less fearful overall, though she is still filthy and too thin.

Perhaps soon I will see her smile. Hear her laughter and her sweet voice for myself.

Until then, I must wait.

I take my kill to my sister's hut, where her mate scrapes hides near their door, his daughter Esha helping him. He looks surprised to see me, and I raise a hand. "Do not get up. I am not staying. I only bring food for my sister's family."

Kashrem frowns, then glances around to see if anyone is near. "I thank you, brother."

I grunt at his polite words and duck into the hut.

As the tribe's healer, Maylak has a slightly larger hut than most, with a small, comfortable area near the front intended for guests who drop in, complaining of aches and pains. Harrec is there now, lounging on furs, his hand extended and his face carefully averted. My sister's fingers press against Harrec's palm, and her eyes are slightly brighter in that way that tells me that she is using her healing. "What did you do this time, Harrec?" I ask as I greet my sister with a tweak to her braids and then head to the slab in the back of her hut where she prepares her food.

"Fish hook," Harrec says, voice faint. He doesn't look at his hand at all; Harrec gets ill at the sight of his own blood. "I was trying to teach Kate how to fish."

I snort at that. The big hunter has made it quite clear that he is interested in Kate, even if she is frustrated by him. I have seen him seated close to her near fires at night. I shake my head. "You will impress her more if you do not faint at your own injury."

"Go away before I shun you," he calls out grumpily, and my sister chuckles. Of all of the tribe, the unmated hunters and my sister do not pay attention to the shunning. They respect the chief's wishes, and I keep my visits brief so as to not put her into an awkward situation, but I make sure to stop by daily.

It is someone to talk to, and sometimes my own thoughts are not enough.

Right now, though, my thoughts are focused on one person and one person alone. "When you are finished, I would speak with you, my sister."

Maylak glances up at me and then nods. "We are done here." She reaches into a small pot and slathers a poultice of crushed herbs over his hand, then wraps a long strip of leather around it. With a pat, she releases him. "Keep that covered for the next day and it should be fine afterward."

"My thanks, healer," he says, shaky as he gets to his feet.

"Go sit near the fire in the long-house until you recover," she tells him in a firm voice. "No matter where Kate is."

Harrec just grins and wobbles out the door.

When the flap drops, she turns to me and gives a little shake of her head. "You would think that someone who hates the sight of his own blood so much would be less clumsy."

"It is Harrec," I say with a shrug, as if that explains it all.

"Mm. What troubles you today, brother?" She washes her hands in a water-bowl and then gets to her feet. Maylak regards me with calm eyes, her manner soothing. She is easy to be around, my sister.

I scrub a hand over my face. "It is my mate—Ell-ee. I worry she is unwell."

"Because she is...small?"

"She is thin. I worry she does not eat. I feel I should be here to take care of her, and yet I cannot stay long because I am forbidden." Just thinking about the unfairness of it makes my fists clench with anger. "It is not right to keep a hunter separated from his mate."

"Perhaps not, but many are still upset over what you did."

I stare at my sister, aghast. "You take their side?"

"I take the tribe's side, brother." Maylak's smile is gentle. "The humans are very sensitive about certain things, and your actions have upset them greatly. When you apologize, all will be forgiven."

I snort. "There is nothing to apologize for. I asked for mates to be brought to our people, and they were brought. If anything, they should be thanking me."

"That is not how the humans see it. And they are just as much a part of our tribe as you."

This is a futile discussion. "I just want to know about Ell-ee. Is she well? Have you treated her?"

Maylak shrugs lightly. "She will not let me touch her. She will not let anyone touch her. Perhaps in time she will trust us, but for now, I must assume that her khui is taking care of her. The other humans are quite healthy, though."

I care nothing for the other humans. Only one consumes my thoughts. "Can you not...do something about that?" I throw my hands up. "Force her to come see you."

"Shall I tackle her to the ground as you did?"

I am in no mood for my sister's teasing. I growl at her and stalk out of her hut, ignoring her faint laughter. I do not like that she is right, but I also do not like that no one seems to be worrying about my mate. Does no one see how fragile Ell-ee is? She is fire and strength in her spirit, but her body does not seem to realize this.

I will just have to stay closer to the village, I realize. Hunt the valley closest to the gorge and remain nearby at all times. Perhaps she is not eating because she does not like the food that is prepared for her. I know the new humans cannot hunt for themselves, so Stay-see and the others feed them the cooked meat they enjoy. Maybe my Ell-ee likes hers raw and full of blood.

I ponder this as I head toward the outskirts of the village, my thoughts full of how to feed and please my mate. I am so wrapped in thoughts of Ell-ee and her big eyes that I nearly step on Erevair as he rushes up to me, little spear in hand. "Bek! There you are!" He looks delighted to see me.

I cannot help myself; I pick him up and swing him into my arms, grinning. I have always thought of this one as my own kit. Perhaps someday soon he will be able to play with my son...or daughter. The thought makes a knot form in my throat. "Where is your mama, Erevair?"

"She is in the long-house. I am playing a game of hide and seek with her."

I can only imagine the terror in Claire's face when she realizes her son has wandered so far away. "You should hide closer to your mama. She will not like you out here by yourself." I poke his round belly. "Or that you are talking to me. I am shunned, you know."

He rolls his eyes with exaggeration. "It is so silly. How can I pretend you are not here when you are?"

Wise words from a kit. I set him down and point at the long-house. "Go. You do not want to get in trouble."

Erevair's small face scrunches up. "You said you would take me hunting soon, remember?"

"I remember," I tell him, and ruffle his hair. His little horns are still not more than nubs, and I wonder if they will always be small because of his human heritage. "But many things have happened, and I cannot keep my promise yet."

"How long do I have to wait?"

"It might be a long time," I admit to him. I do not know how long it will take for Vektal—and the humans—to forgive my actions, especially when I am not sorry for them. I cannot pretend something I do not feel.

"How long is a long time?"

I see a glimpse of Ell-ee in the archway of the long-house, and my khui begins to purr. Hot need pours through me. "I must go."

"Where are you going?"

"Back to the hunter cave I am living in," I tell him absently, though I doubt I will go that far. I will make a camp closer, I think, so I can be close to Ell-ee. Perhaps by the dirt-beak nests...but they squawk all night long and smell terrible. Perhaps not.

"If I come to your cave, can you take me hunting?"

"Of course," I tell him, my mind on other things. I ruffle his hair again. "But it will be a long time before your mama allows that." I give him a gentle nudge toward the long-house. "Go surprise her. Show her how clever you are by finding her first."

He grins at me and races back toward the long-house, pleased at the change in his game. I rub my chest, ignoring the ache in my heart—and the one in my groin—as Ell-ee pauses in the doorway, gazing out at me. She says nothing and makes no gesture that she sees me.

But I think she does. My khui sings a little louder, and I remind myself that they cannot keep us apart forever.

Patience.

8

ELLY

The stew simmering on the fire smells incredible. I can't make myself walk away, even though I know I won't eat a bite. Stacy's making it for freezing in mine and Gail's hut's cold storage, and that means no one else will be taking a mouthful. That means it's not safe. I'm so hungry, but I can't make myself ask for a bowl. I wish I were braver, and then maybe my stomach wouldn't feel as if it's gnawing itself from the inside.

Stacy and Claire sit by the fire, nursing their younger children as they talk. Nora and an elder named Vadren sit nearby, making nets with the help of a few of the older children. Gail isn't around—Vaza showed up with a pile of plants in his arms and said something about "No Poison" and kissing, and I left the hut fast. I think Gail likes all the attention Vaza gives her, and he treats her well. He doesn't seem to mind that she won't resonate.

I'm envious of Gail. She's happy, and she doesn't have to worry about resonating. I rub my own chest, feeling betrayed by my cootie. Did it have to pick someone out so fast? Couldn't it have given me time? No one else has even come close to resonating—just me. The others are free to flirt and go about to their heart's content.

My stomach knots up as I think of Bek. The moment I think of him, I get aroused. I don't know what to do about it, and it feels like it gets worse every day. He watches me from afar when I'm in the village, but instead of making me feel weird, it makes me feel...seen.

No one else notices me, not really. Gail tries to include me, but it's hard to include someone when they don't speak. I'm just like a dirty shadow lingering on the sidelines. Even now, I'm in the main long-house by the fire, and there are other women here, and I don't feel included. I know all it would take is a word or two, but I can't make those words come out of my throat. I want to have friends, too. I just...can't make myself say anything to them. So I lurk and smile when they smile at me, and that's it.

But Bek sees me. He doesn't make me feel forgotten. He makes me feel like I have a spotlight on me...and sometimes I think I hate it.

Sometimes I don't.

I still war with feeling safe here. Even though the others reassure me that no aliens are coming back, that we're not slaves, I feel lost. Alone. Having Bek nearby helps, strangely enough. It's like he's got my back. Gail's nice, and we're friends—as much as I have any friends—but she couldn't protect me from the slavers.

Bek could.

I hate that I find him appealing even after all of this. I'm sure a lot of it is the cootie's influence on me. It wants us to make babies, so it's going to do its best to make sure that I think about making babies all the time. And boy, do I think about sex a lot. But it's more than that, I think. It's the way Bek walked at my side without trying to grab me. He hasn't said anything about my dirt or tried to push me into having sex. It's like he's waiting for me to realize he's right there. That it's my call, even if my cootie's already decided.

And that raises him a notch or two in my mind.

"I want to go see Bek, Mama," a little voice says, and I'm drawn out of my thoughts. I look over and see it's Erevair, holding his little spear and tugging on the hem of his mother's tunic. "You said I could."

"Not right now, baby," Claire tells him, switching Relvi to her other breast and adjusting her tunic. "Mama's busy. Go play with Anna and Elsa." It's clear she's not listening to him, because her attention is focused on Stacy, who's whispering about something in a low voice. A secret, perhaps.

"Mama," Erevair says again. "Bek said I could see him in his cave. Can I go?"

Claire glances over at her son and smooths his messy hair. "Erevair, honey, I said go play with Anna and Elsa, okay?"

"Can I go?" he asks again.

The baby at Claire's breast starts to cry, and her attention is drawn to it. She fusses over her daughter, even as Erevair continues to yank on her tunic.

"Mama," he says again, a whine in his voice.

"Yes, yes, you can go," Claire tells him absently as the baby continues to hiccup and cry. "Just go play."

A look of delight crosses Erevair's face, and he runs out of the long-house. I watch him go, curious. He seemed eager to see Bek—does that mean Bek likes children? Why does the thought make me feel warm inside? I can't even imagine having a child of my own, but I like the thought of someone as big and strong—and capable of brutality—as Bek being kind and patient with little kids.

Maybe he'd be kind and patient with me, too.

Disgusted that I even entertain the thought, I get to my feet and head for my hut. Maybe I'll see if Gail and Vaza have finished making out and I can go take a nap.

"Erevair?" Claire's frantic voice rouses me from a restless nap.

I sit up in my furs, rubbing at my eyes, and glance around. I'm alone in the hut I share with Gail. The fire's out, and it's dark in here, but not so dark that it means that it's nighttime.

"Erevair? Where are you, baby? Come out. Mama's tired of playing." Claire's voice is so loud it hurts my ears. She must be standing right outside of the hut.

I slip my boots on and pull my fur wraps over my body, then head outside. There are people everywhere, which makes me shrink back a little, and everyone seems to be combing the village looking for something. Claire stands near my door, her hands cupped to her mouth, her face pale and pinched.

"Erevair?" she calls again, and then notices me. "Oh. Elly. You haven't seen Erevair, have you?" Her lower lip wobbles. "I think he's playing hide and seek again, but I can't find him."

Behind her, Georgie, Stacy, and Marlene are checking inside other huts, and I see Gail and Vaza opening the lids of baskets. Everyone's looking for Erevair.

I shake my head at Claire, wishing I had better news for her.

She nods slowly and gives a loud sniff. "If you see him, please tell him I'm looking for him." She wanders away a little further and then cups her hands to her mouth again. "EREVAIR!"

With a sick feeling, I remember the little boy's conversation from earlier. He wanted to find Bek. I wonder if Claire realizes this. She'd been distracted. I look around the village, searching for a familiar large blue form that always seems to be lurking a short distance away when I'm out, but Bek is nowhere to be seen.

He must be hunting.

I rack my brain, trying to recall what Erevair had said about visiting him. Something about...a cave? I should tell Claire. I hurry forward and try to get her attention. She turns to me, worry and stress stamped on her features. "What is it?"

I open my mouth to speak...but nothing comes out. The words are lodged in my throat. Oh god. I can't do it. I want to, but I can't. It's like my brain is totally blocked. Nothing comes out but a squeak.

Claire bites her lip. "What is it, Elly?" She looks around, twitchy and impatient, and I know she wants nothing more than to find her child.

And I'm sitting here, mute and unhelpful. I shake my head.

"I'm sorry, but I have to find Erevair," she tells me, already rushing past.

I'm filled with guilt. What is wrong with me? Why can't I speak out loud to save a child? I feel like the worst person imaginable. Maybe I've forgotten how to speak because it's been so long.

I need to do something to help, though. I walk away, thoughtful, trying to recall more of what Erevair said. It was all about Bek and wanting to spend time with him. There was a cave mentioned. Where is there a cave around here, then?

I find myself walking to the pulley at the far end of the canyon. I'll just pull myself up and see if there are tracks out there. If there are, I'll go to the others and try to sign-language it out or something. Heck, I'll draw stick figures if I can't spit the words out. I'll do something to help out. But first I need to be sure I'm not just making things worse.

So I walk to the pulley, my steps quick. I must be more tired than usual, because even that short walk—no more than ten minutes—seems to sap all of my energy. I'm so incredibly weak, my feet feel like they're sandbags. I pause and rub my neck, catching my breath, and my stomach churns. Maybe I should have eaten something.

Maybe you should have said something to Claire, my brain reminds me, *instead of running off half-cocked.*

I'm already here, though. The pulley's just a short distance ahead, and I'll see if there are footprints, and then I'll go back to the village. Grimly determined, I ignore my fatigue and push through, moving slowly to the pulley. It's hard to tell if anyone's been here in the last hour or two, which means I'll need to go up. I stand on the pulley and grab the rope, then begin to tug myself upward.

Even though I'm tired, the pulley is easy to use and requires little muscle work, so I'm at the top in no time. I step off and release the rope, and it slides back down to the ground below. Whoops. I should have secured it, and now I'm going to have to pull it back up again. My brain's a little foggy, though. I'll worry about that later.

I take a few steps forward into the snow. The landscape up here looks completely different than down below. The gorge is protected from the worst of the weather, but up here, the snow is thick. Sunlight glints off of it, and rolling white hills lead to distant trees and even more distant purple mountains. The skies are bright blue, and a few puffy white clouds dot the otherwise clear sky. It's...so pretty. So open. I love it.

In this moment, I want to take up hunting, just so I can come out and enjoy this every day.

The snow here is thick, though, and at the pulley station, it's heavily churned from many feet. It's impossible to tell which ones are recent, so I look for small footprints instead of big ones. Sure enough, one set is of feet smaller than my own, leading off into the hills. I follow it, fatigued and dizzy.

It takes a few minutes for it to sink in that I shouldn't be following the trail. That I should be heading back to the village to let them know that I've seen footprints. But...I'm this far in. What if he's just over the next rise? I could retrieve him and bring him home and ease everyone's worries. Turning around now seems foolish...and exhausting, too. I'm so tired.

So I walk on. I'm in over my head, I think. It seemed like such a simple thing—go to pulley, find footprints, return—but I seem to be messing everything up. It's because I can't think straight. There are stars at the edges of my vision, and my focus tunnels until I can see nothing but the footsteps in the snow in front of me.

Through my grogginess, I notice that there's a second set of footprints that have appeared next to the small ones. Huh.

"Ell-ee?"

I look up, the action of lifting my head making the world tilt crazily. I really, really should have eaten something. I really should have stayed in the village. My gaze focuses slowly, and two blurry figures straighten into one lumpy one.

It's Bek, and Erevair's in his arms.

"Safe," I croak out. The black tunnel creeping into my vision grows thicker, and I feel myself topple forward. The last conscious thought I have is that it looks like I haven't forgotten to talk after all.

BEK

Out of all the things I expect to see on the trails on a quiet morning, little Erevair is not one of them. I am hunched down by one of my traps, resetting it carefully, when I hear a small, piping voice behind me. "Bek!"

I whip around in surprise, startled to see Claire's son racing toward me as fast as he can in the thick snow. He has the little spear I made him in hand, his fur cape flapping behind him, a big grin on his face.

And I am immediately sick with fear at the sight of him. Had I not seen metlak tracks in this area just a few moons ago? And is he not the right size for a snow-cat to feast upon? A sky-claw? There are any number of predators that could pick off a small kit, not to mention the dangers of deep snow, ice-covered crevasses, and a number of other elements that a smart hunter knows to look for. "Erevair. What are you doing?" I rush to him and snatch him into my arms, holding him close. My heart thuds heavy in my chest. Luck watches over him this day.

"I came to see you," Erevair tells me happily, throwing his arms around my neck. "Now we can hunt."

"Where is your mama? Your papa?" I return his hug and then look him in the eye, though I want to shake sense into him. "Are they with you?"

"I came alone," he tells me proudly, confirming my fears. "Mama said I could."

"I doubt that very much," I tell him with a pat on the back. My heart is still pounding, and I can only imagine how worried Claire is. "Does she know you are here?" His silence tells me everything. "I see. Let us go back to the village. You cannot hunt with me this day."

"But why not?" he whines, disappointed. "I want to hunt with you."

"Another time," I tell him, and cannot resist giving him another hug. He is safe; Claire will be so thankful. "For now, we must take you back to your mama. She will be worried that you are gone."

He protests and pouts, but when I promise we will check a few traps as we return, he ceases to complain. I hurry my steps through the valley, trying not to clutch him too close to my chest out of fear and relief. I will have to talk to Ereven about how we can keep Erevair occupied. Perhaps he needs a task given to himself that only a small kit can do. I remember when I was young, my task was to set out my father's weapons every day and check them with him. I know Ereven does something similar with Erevair, but maybe the kit needs more to occupy him. We pass by one of my traps, and there is a fresh quill-beast caught in the snare, and Erevair is beside himself with excitement at bringing home fresh meat for his mama. I reset the trap quickly, scoop the kit up into my arms again, and continue hurrying back to the canyon.

As I do, I see a fur-covered figure up ahead. At first I think it is one of the hunters, but as I approach, I realize the form is too small, the movements too unsteady. Claire alone, then? What foolishness is this? I bite back my scowl and hug Erevair a little closer as I jog through the snow, rushing to get to her.

It is only when my khui begins to sing that I realize who it is staggering ahead of me. "Ell-ee?"

She looks up, and her face is as pale as the snow, her eyes bright blue and enormous in her face. "Safe," she says, and then slumps to the ground.

I let out a hoarse shout of fear and rush to her side, setting Erevair down carefully in the snow and then cradling my mate to my chest. I brush her filthy hair back from her face, scarcely daring to breathe as I trail my fingers over her cheek. She breathes. I exhale with relief, the crushing fear in my chest easing a bit.

"Is Elly all right?" Erevair asks in a small voice. "She looks sick."

She does look sick, and my heart hurts at how light she is. "I do not know."

"Mama says she doesn't eat enough."

I have noticed this also. "I will make her eat," I vow to him.

He holds out his freshly trapped quill-beast. "Do you want her to eat this? I can share."

I feel a surge of love for this small kit. "You are a generous hunter," I tell him gravely. "But let us wake Ell-ee first." He hunches down in the snow next to me, and we watch my mate's face, waiting. She seems to be sleeping peacefully, her breathing regular. Is she faint because she did not eat enough? Surely my khui would know she cannot mate if she is sick, and it hums in my chest as urgent as ever. I cradle her close to my chest, worried.

She moans and stirs, and I resist the urge to squeeze her tight against me. I never want to let her go. Her eyes flutter open after a moment, and she gazes up at me, our khuis humming in perfect time. And I tell her the first thing I think of. "Safe," I whisper. "You're safe with me."

Ell-ee gives a little sigh, and to my surprise, settles back in against me, tucking her face against my vest. Her hand curls around the leather of my clothing, and she holds on to me. I feel a surge of pleasure rush through me that she would trust me so, and I vow not to disappoint her. I get to my feet, making sure my mate is protected in my arms, and glance down at Erevair. "Are you a big enough hunter to be able to walk back to the village?"

He nods proudly. "Can I carry my kill since you are carrying Elly?"

"Of course." I feel a surge of pride as he squares his small shoulders and begins to march ahead of me. This is a strange day. First Erevair, then Ell-ee. I am relieved that both are safe, and a small part of me is secretly glad, because now I get to hold my mate close.

I glance down at her as I walk, feeling protective, and her eyes are closed, her breathing even. I wonder if she is pretending sleep, but I decide it does not matter. If she is trusting me enough to let me touch her, it is enough for now. She will give me more in her own time.

The walk is a brief one compared to my normal hunting treks —just through the valley itself—but Erevair begins to tire after a short time. I watch him as his steps slow, wondering how I am going to carry both child and mate, because I refuse to leave either behind. To my relief, I spot a figure up ahead, and the tangle of shoulder-length mane tells me that it is Erevair's father. Not wanting to frighten my mate with a call of greeting to Ereven, I hold up a hand instead. "There is your father, Erevair."

The other hunter gives a shout, and Ell-ee jerks in my arms, her eyes flying open with fear, body tense.

"Shh. All is well," I murmur to her, but set her down gently. It pains me to release her because I want to hold her close, and I feel a surge of pride when she steps behind me, using me as a shield. She wants me to protect her. I like this. She is mine, and it makes my khui's song even stronger.

Ereven drops to his knees and pulls his little son into his arms. Sheer joy and relief are carved into his face as he hugs Erevair close. "My son, my son, where have you been? Your mother has been crying all afternoon."

Erevair's little face crumples. "Am I in trouble, Papa? I just wanted to go hunting with Bek." He holds up the frozen quill-beast, which has been dragged along in the snow and looks worse for its journey.

"No trouble," Ereven says, ruffling his son's hair. "But you must go home and apologize to your mama for scaring her so." He glances up at me, and his face seems as if it has aged overnight. "You found him?"

I nod. "I think he slipped away when Claire was busy. I ran into him while checking my traps."

"I just wanted to hunt," Erevair says again, with the innocence only a child has.

"You can hunt with me very soon," Ereven promises, lifting him into his arms. "But for now, we must get you home." He pulls his son close and presses a fierce kiss on his brow. "You have made my mane go gray with worry."

Erevair giggles. "It's still dark and messy, Papa."

"Just wait until tomorrow." He grins over at me, relief stark, his shoulders a little straighter. "Is that Ell-ee behind you? Claire said that Ell-ee tried to tell her something, but she would not speak. Claire said when she looked for Ell-ee again, she was gone."

I glance over at Ell-ee, but she averts her eyes, seemingly not interested in answering for herself. I think of Ereven's words—she did not speak to Claire, but she spoke to me. My pride surges, and I can practically feel my chest puff up. "Ell-ee guessed where Erevair went and came after him."

"This is all of our worries solved, then. Both missing people found." Ereven's grin is tired, and he presses another fatherly kiss to his boy's mane. "I will tell Vektal of your help today."

"Bah." As if I care what that one thinks. Being leader has made him sour.

"I will," Ereven continues. "Not everyone agrees with this shunning foolishness."

It is just gratitude that makes Ereven so eager to take my side, I think. I shrug and pretend not to be pleased by his loyalty. "Vektal does what he feels is best for the tribe. He feels I broke rules, so he must act or else there is no point in having a leader." Huh. This might be the first time I have thought about it that way...and suddenly I feel less resentment for my chief. Of course he is being strict. First Raahosh steals Leezh, then Hassen steals Li-lah. He likely thinks I am acting as foolish as them.

My actions were deliberate, though. I did not care about the consequences, and I bear them now, happily, because I have a mate.

Or at least, I will when Ell-ee finally comes to accept me.

I will still not apologize for having Trakan steal her and the others, however. So I shrug at Ereven. "You do not have to say anything to Vektal on my behalf."

"So be it, my friend." He peers around me, looking at Ell-ee. "Shall I take you back to the village?"

I glance back at my mate, who even now hovers behind me, her posture timid. She looks at me and then at Ereven. After a moment's hesitation, she slips her hand in mine.

Did I think I was full of joy before? There is nothing that compares to her small, soft fingers brushing against my skin. My cock immediately reacts, and I bite back my groan of pleasure. I will stroke my cock to this tonight, just the simple act of her hand in mine. It will be more than enough to make me come with great force.

I cannot think about that right now, or I will rip off my loincloth and begin.

"So you choose to stay?" Ereven asks. "I mean you no harm if it is me you are afraid of."

"Safe," she whispers, so low that only I can hear it. And she presses closer to me.

I nod. I know what she is asking. "I will keep you safe with me. Have no fear." I make no move to touch her, letting my skittish mate decide how much she can handle. If all she wants is her hand held, I will give her that, even if I long to crush her against my chest with every whispered word she gives me. I turn to Ereven. "Ell-ee wishes to stay."

"Ell-ee?" Ereven asks. "Are you certain?"

She nods. Just once. Her free hand creeps to my vest, and she clings to my leathers.

He grunts acknowledgment. "I will tell the others so they do not worry over you. Where is it you sleep these days, Bek?"

I keep my movements slow so as not to frighten my mate. "The hunter cave over the rise. The small one."

"Very well. Safe journey to you and your mate, brother." He hesitates, as if uncertain about leaving Ell-ee with me, but then Erevair puts his head down on his father's shoulder and yawns, and it decides him. He raises a hand to tell me he is leaving and then turns in the snow, carrying his son back to the village and his waiting mother.

And I am here. Alone.

With my mate.

Today is a day of great joy.

9

ELLY

Pretty sure that passing out all the time around Bek is going to earn me the reputation of a lightweight. I feel silly about that as he turns to look at me. He probably thinks I'm one stiff wind away from shattering into a thousand pieces. Somehow that's okay, though. It feels like it's all right to be a little fragile around him.

Which is strange.

I feel a little silly and weak for passing out on him. That's total damsel-in-distress stuff, and I like to view myself as stronger than that. But it's my own fault—I haven't been eating. What dummy does that? This one, I guess. It's my own pigheaded fear that gets me into these messes. When I wake up and find myself cradled against his chest, though? And he tells me I'm safe?

It's weird, but I believe him. I do feel safe. Wrapped in his arms, burrowed against his warm body, I feel like the most protected woman in the world. Instead of fighting to get away from him, I let myself sink against him and close my eyes. I'm going to trust him. If he betrays me, I'll never forgive him, but for now, I'm going to trust.

I lie in his arms and let him hold me, and it feels…so good. Too good. I can feel my cootie purring in my breast and the slippery ache starting between my legs again. I've been abused so many times in the past that I expect him to pull a trick of some kind or to grab me. But he doesn't. He just holds me. Even when Ereven appears and Bek sets me down, he doesn't grab at me. And so I trust him a bit more.

Safe, he said. I'm going out on a limb and trusting that, even though I have no reason to. My cootie thinks he's good, though, and he doesn't grab, which puts him ahead of so many others.

It's funny, too, because a week ago, I wouldn't have wanted to be anywhere near Bek. Not after his brutal tackle after the hunt. I thought then that he was awful, but his behavior in the days since has made me wonder. He's been patient but present, persistent but still giving me my own space. It's like he knows I need time to adjust to things and he's willing to give it to me.

As someone who's been pushed and shoved by others for most of her life, I appreciate this more than anything.

So when Ereven asks if I want to return to the village with him, I hesitate. He's Claire's mate, and I know he doesn't mean me any harm. He's always smiling and happy and one of the friendliest of the tribe. But…I feel safe with Bek. It's weird, but I feel safer standing behind him in the snow than I do with Gail in our little hut. It's like…when I'm at his side, I know he won't let anything happen to me.

I put my hand in his. Bek's skin is warmer than mine, with a velvety softness to it despite the calluses on his hand. I thought touching him would make me feel uncomfortable, but if anything, it makes me feel better. I like it. I want to press my face up against his back and slip a hand under his vest, just to press my skin against his. But I'm not that brave yet.

"So you choose to stay?" Ereven asks. "I mean you no harm if it is me you are afraid of."

"Safe," I tell Bek, and he nods slowly. He doesn't touch me, either, and I am grateful. Maybe it's not the wisest idea to stay out here with him, but I want to. *What's the worst that can happen?* I ask myself. He'll betray me? He'll collar me and put me in a cage? I've been there before, and I lived through it. All I know is that if I go back to the village, I won't have this big warm hand to hold, and this safe feeling will go away. I hadn't realized until now just how hungry I've been for the feeling of shelter, of having someone to fall back on.

I don't want to let it go. I don't want to let his hand go, either. Maybe it's the exhaustion, but the thought of leaving his side and returning to the village holds zero appeal to me.

Ereven leaves, and then it's just me and Bek. He turns and faces me, his expression thoughtful. "Should you go back to the village, Ell-ee? Are you feeling unwell? My sister is the healer, and she can help. I promise she will not touch you more than she has to."

I shake my head, resisting the urge to hide under my dirty curtain of hair. I don't want to go back. I'm tired, and I like my hand in his.

"I worry about you," he chides me. "You fainted."

I swallow hard and then make an eating gesture with my free hand.

"Not eating?" There's a rumble in his tone like disapproval. "You are too thin as it is. Do you not like the food?"

I stare mutely at the ground. I tug on his hand. Can't we please just go to his fire and sit? I can't explain why I don't eat certain things. He'll think I'm stupid. Just like he probably already thinks I'm stupid because I smell bad and am dirty.

For the first time, I wonder if he's...disappointed in his cootie picking me as a mate. I hate that I'm even wondering that. I shouldn't care. It's not like I want him to touch me or kiss me.

But I do like his hand in mine, an awful lot.

He doesn't seem to mind that I've gotten all quiet on him again. He just squeezes my hand—which startles me—and doesn't press. "My cave is this way. Are you well enough to walk?"

Am I? I don't know. I keep my hand in his and take a few steps forward. I do think I'm strong enough to walk, but I'm so damn tired. It's like all of my energy is gone, and there's two feet of snow on the ground to wade through. Lifting each foot feels like massive effort.

"You are tired," Bek says, and his voice is gentle—gentler than I've ever heard it. "Let me carry you. I am strong." When I hesitate, he continues. "I will never drop you, Ell-ee. Never." The fervent tone in his voice has me believing him.

I nod, pulling my hand from his and then waiting.

Warm arms go around me, one sliding under my thighs. I'm startled at the contact, and it's like I can feel his touch all the way through my leathers. My gaze flicks to his, and our eyes meet for a long, awkward moment.

My pulse starts beating between my thighs again, and I feel flushed and hot. My cootie is so loud that my entire body feels like it's vibrating along with it. Oh. I press a hand to my chest to try and calm it.

"Ignore it," he tells me with a wry voice. "That is what I do." And he scoops me up and tucks me against his shoulder as if I weigh nothing.

And...okay. It's been years and years since I've seen a movie, but I remember the hero always grabbing the heroine and picking her up as if she weighs nothing. That's what I feel like right now—a princessy heroine who's just been rescued.

Even if it means I was rescued from my own silliness, it's kind of nice. And he's warm, and safe. I lean a little closer to him and notice that when I do, I can smell the spicy, clean scent of his skin and hear his heartbeat through the purr of his cootie. It just makes me want to snuggle closer.

God, to think I'm even contemplating snuggling with Bek. Bek, of all people. The mean one. The one that tackled me to the ground so unforgivably after the sa-kohtsk hunt. The one that grabbed me and brought me back to the ship. The one that bought slaves.

Except he hasn't treated me like a slave yet. Maybe that's why I'm all confused. I keep waiting for a collar, a slap, something.

But he only holds me close.

We're both silent as he carries me across the snow, but it's not an awkward silence. At least, it doesn't feel awkward to me. He seems content to not fill the air with mindless chatter, and of course, I have nothing to say. Even if I was comfortable enough to chatter endlessly like Josie, I'm not sure I'd have anything to say anyhow. Silence is easier, because the other person will rush to fill it. You can learn more about someone when they volunteer information. But Bek's as quiet as I am.

It feels as if he's been walking forever, and I wonder if I should protest and walk the rest of the way to help out, when he says a quiet, "We are here. Can you walk?"

I nod and slide out of his arms, though I feel unsteady on the ground. He puts an arm around my waist automatically, and I stiffen.

"I am not going to let you fall," he tells me in a firm voice. "You need support, and I know you do not want to be touched, but I am not going to let my mate land on the ground when I can help out."

He's right, of course. I'm being skittish. If it was anyone else, I would have gone after them with teeth and nails already...but Bek is safe. I don't know how I know that, I just do. So I let his arm stay as I wobble a few feet, trying to get my balance. When I'm good, I push at his arm.

Bek lets me go, but gives me a fierce look and hands me his spear. "Stay right here. Use this to support you. I am going to clear the cave to make sure it is safe."

Is there a chance it's not safe? I worry about that, but he disappears inside and then comes back out again within moments. "It is safe." At my expression, he continues. "Sometimes a creature will come inside seeking shelter from the cold. I did not want to risk your safety."

Oh. That makes sense. Using his spear as a crutch, I wobble inside after him.

The cave itself isn't huge. When I think of caves, I think of one that I visited with my parents when I was a child—full of stalactites and stalagmites and walkways for tourists. This one's just a mere nook in the side of a snow-covered hill, long and thin and not very wide. As I step inside, Bek crouches near a firepit and sparks rocks over tinder until a small flame starts. He builds it up while I stand awkwardly, and then he gets to his feet and begins to move around the cave. As I watch, he unties a few rolls of fur, spreading them out near the fire and indicating I should sit. From there, he puts away his weapons, sets a pouch for hot water over the fire, and then kneels next to me, gesturing at my sodden boots.

Right. Leaving my feet in soggy fur boots will only make them turn into blocks of ice. I reach for the laces that crisscross up the calf, and my fingers shake.

"Let me," he murmurs in a low voice. "You rest."

I fight against the urge to slap his hands away. He's trying to be helpful. It's just...hard for me to accept help without thinking there is something else that is going to be asked for in the future, a favor called in. Obedience demanded. I let my hands fall away, and then he takes over, carefully undoing the knots and making sure he does not touch me more than he has to. There's no sound in the cave except for the crackle of the small fire and the endless singing of our khuis.

And then my boots are off and my pruney toes are free. I wiggle them and move nearer to the fire. I pull off my outer wraps, and I'm not surprised when Bek moves to my side and helps me. One thing I've learned about living on the ice planet, it's that when you go outside for any length of time, there's a constant removing of sodden layers of clothing to exchange them for new layers of clothing. I remove my outer layers and then huddle closer to the fire, because it's warm enough inside the cave that I don't need to throw more blankets on until the suns go down and the temperature drops.

"You should not have come after Erevair," he tells me as he takes my fur wraps and spreads them out to dry. "Bravery is ill-placed when one is as weak as you are."

Oh, is it time for the lecture now? Lucky me. I snort to let him know I heard his words and extend my hands to the fire. My stomach rumbles and hurts, but I'm paying more attention to the cootie in my chest that's humming non-stop. It's making me feel strange, like exhausted and turned on at the same time. It's really not a fun combination.

"It is true," Bek insists, and then goes to one of the storage baskets at the back of the cave and pulls out a pouch. He moves to sit next to me by the fire, folding his legs under him with incredible grace given his size. His tail flicks on the furs, close to me but not too close, and he offers me the pouch. "Trail rations. It is not much, but I am not leaving you to go hunting until I know you are well."

I stare at the pouch, torn. I'm starving and still shaky, and I know that eating will help, but my stomach twists into a knot just thinking about it. What if...what if this is a trick?

Bek's jaw clenches when I don't reach for the food. He shakes it at me and then gives me an exasperated look. "Do you not like trail rations?"

I would eat cardboard right now. My stomach growls, betraying my thoughts, and Bek narrows his eyes at me. "Eat."

I swallow hard, because my mouth is watering. Everything in me wants desperately to eat, but I can't force myself to reach for the food.

"Ell-ee," he growls in his throat.

I know. I know I'm being ridiculous and scared. I fight back tears of frustration. Does he think I want to starve myself? I want to tell him off, to point out that I'm not stupid, but the knot in my throat won't let me speak.

"This is ridiculous," he says, words biting with frustration. "Do I need to eat a bite to show you how to do so?"

My head jerks up and I give him a look of hope.

His eyes widen. "Is that it? You need me to eat it first?" When I bite my lip, he takes one of the ration cakes and takes a hearty bite out of it, chewing, then offers me the pouch.

I reach out and snatch the bitten one out of his hand and cram it into my mouth, chewing so fast that crumbs are flying down the front of my leather tunic. I don't care. I just want to eat. The taste of it is extra spicy, like the sa-khui prefer their food, but it's delicious. I try to swallow and cough on the mouthful.

Bek hands me a waterskin and then hesitates, takes a sip out of it, and then offers it to me.

I shoot him a grateful look even as I grab it out of his hands and take a big sip.

"Eat slower," he commands me. "It does no good if the food does not reach your stomach." He pulls another cake out of the pouch, takes a bite out of it, and then offers it to me.

It takes everything I have not to snatch it away again. I force myself to take it from him gently, to take small bites. No one is here to snatch it away from me. I can take my time if I need to. I sip more water and nibble at the cake. My stomach hurts from putting food into it, but I'm not going to stop eating.

Bek just watches me as I chew. When I finish my cake, he takes a bite out of another and gives it to me, and we repeat the process twice more until he puts the pouch away. "I would give you more, but if you have not been eating, you will get sick. We will have tea, and then more cakes when your stomach can handle it."

It makes sense. I don't protest as he gets up and puts fresh-scooped snow into the boiling pouch, then adds a sprinkle of leaves. "Is this why you are not eating, Ell-ee? Because you feel others must eat your food first?" He looks over at me, his gaze intense.

I don't know how to explain to him, to make him understand. My throat knots up again, and I shrug.

"Is it because you feel the food is bad?" When I don't respond, he continues to guess. "Something else? You do not trust the food?" At my tiny nod, he looks surprised. "Has someone given you food and taken it away before?"

I gaze down at my hands. There are still remnants of grease on my fingers, and I have to fight the urge to lick them, because my fingers are filthy. All of me is filthy.

Bek moves to my side and crouches low next to me. He extends his hand, and I look at him in surprise. He just sits there, waiting, and I know what he wants. I suck in a breath, trying to be brave, and put my hand in his. His fingers grip mine, and his hand is warm. Reassuring.

"Did someone give you bad food in the past, Ell-ee? Is that why you won't eat unless I do?"

With his hand holding mine, the knot in my throat loosens a little. "Sick," I tell him in a near whisper. "To make me sick."

His nostrils flare, and I shrink back at his anger.

"Who would try to make you sick? Why?"

I lick my lips, trying to be brave. "They thought it was funny."

His expression grows tight. "What is funny?"

Oh, it's hard to use words after hiding away from them for so long. I shrink into myself, not wanting to explain. It's hard to say things aloud, because a small, hard part of me still worries that my words will be used against me. But then Bek's thumb strokes over the back of my hand, and I feel a little better. "Humans...when we get sick, we vomit or sweat. Make faces. I had an owner that...he thought it was funny to watch. He would trick me by giving me good food one day, and then something bad the next." I swallow hard, because I can still feel the burn in my throat from those days, the taste of vomit on my tongue. I want more water...but I also don't want to pull my hand from Bek's comforting one.

His thumb strokes the back of my hand again. "So you eat... only when someone else eats before you?"

I nod slowly. "Safe."

BEK

Her words make my heart feel as if it is being ripped apart.

Who would do such a thing? Who would make a female sick just to watch her vomit? Give her bad food to make her ill? It makes no sense to me. I do not understand this at all, but I know Ell-ee does not lie. The answer is in her big, haunted eyes and too-thin face.

I want to crush her against me and stroke her hair. My mate has been hurt in the past. If she lived in a place where even the food was not safe...no wonder she does not trust. No wonder she is afraid to eat. No wonder she looks at everything with such fear in her eyes.

And yet...this makes her quiet strength all the more remarkable. Of course she tries to run away. I think of Trakan and his collar and feel sick to my stomach. I think of the way I leapt upon her after the sa-kohtsk hunt and held her down so she could get her khui. It was for the best...but will Ell-ee see it like that?

I rub my thumb over the back of her small hand. So soft. So fragile. Even this small touch feels like a gift. Every whispered word, a treasure.

No one will ever hurt my Ell-ee again. That she is here with me is enough for now. We will take it slow.

"Would you like some tea?" I ask her. When she looks hesitant, I get to my feet and take my favorite bone cup out of my pack, the one my mother made for me when I was a small kit. It is one of the few things I have left of her, and I have never let another touch it. I scoop it into the hot tea and then lift the cup to my lips, taking a sip before offering it to my mate.

She gently takes the cup from my hands and puts it to her lips. Her eyes close, and her expression is one of such pleasure that it makes my cock swell even as my chest aches. "Good?" I ask, voice husky. At her little nod, I mentally note the mixture of tea leaves and decide I will make sure she has it every day for the rest of her life.

Ell-ee finishes her tea slowly, and I refill her cup (after taking a sip of it myself). The pallor is gone from her cheeks, and they seem to be rosy underneath the layer of dirt. At first, I thought she was dirty because she was slovenly, but now I wonder. Is the dirt another thing she has learned because of her past? The other humans are quick to take advantage of bathing, but Ell-ee does not. I vow to find out, but it will take more time. And I will not rush her. She can have all of the time she needs, my sweet mate.

I will be at her side making sure she is safe and protected through all of it.

After she drinks her tea, she seems reluctant to talk more. That is fine; she has said more words to me than she has said to anyone else in all of the days she has been here. I take a bite from another cake of trail rations and offer it to her, and she devours it eagerly. I try not to stare at her as she eats, but it is not easy. I want to devour her features, want to memorize them for every small detail. Will she smile if she eats something sweetly pleasant, like the hraku the other humans are so fond of? I decide I will get some for her, along with fresh meat. Not today, though. I am not leaving her side.

She finishes the cake and fights a yawn.

"Lie down and rest," I tell her, picking up my spear and settling across from her, the fire between us. "I need to sharpen my weapons for tomorrow's hunting."

Ell-ee pulls the furs close to her and props her head up on one arm. Her eyes close, and I watch her for a moment before picking up my sharpening stone and running it along the thin bone edge of my spearhead.

"Can I go with you? Tomorrow?"

Her words are so soft I think I imagine them for a moment, but when I look up, she is watching me.

"Hunting?" I am surprised she asks.

Ell-ee nods. "I like...outside."

"Then we shall go together, if you are strong enough."

She nods again and closes her eyes.

I DO NOT SLEEP much that night. I am too afraid that I will wake and Ell-ee will be gone. That this will all be a dream and when I open my eyes, I will be as alone as before. But she stays, and in the morning, she awakens, her eyes a little brighter than before. I smile at her and do not even mind her ripe scent because it tells me that she is here. I do not mind that her dirty fingers brush over mine, because we are touching.

I make Ell-ee tea, and we have more cakes for breakfast. She seems stronger this day, her expression more alert, and once we finish eating she pulls on her boots and begins to lace them to her calves, readying to go out.

"You are strong enough?" I ask her. "Not feeling faint?"

She gives me a firm little nod that tells me she's fine, and so I put the fire out and ready my weapons.

"Ho," someone calls from outside the cave.

Ell-ee stiffens. I want to groan in annoyance. It is my chief. If he has come to steal my mate away from me, I will... I look at her small form, her eyes wide, and I blow out a breath of frustration. I will let her go, I suppose, because I do not wish to alarm her. "Wait here," I tell her. "It is Vektal. I will see what he wants."

She gives me a little nod and remains in the furs, waiting by the firepit.

I emerge from the cave and head out to greet my chief. Vektal has a pack on his back and his oldest daughter, Talie, with him.

I am happy to see that—it means this visit will be both friendly and brief. "My chief," I greet him.

"Bek," he greets me evenly. "I should like to speak to you for a moment."

It is on the tip of my tongue to ask if he is not shunning me this day, but I do not wish to be unpleasant in front of a kit. "Of course." I smile at Talie, who looks more like Shorshie than her father today, her brown curls tied up in two twists atop her head. "Ell-ee is inside the cave. Will you go say hello to her?"

"Of course," Talie says in that direct, firm tone I have heard from Shorshie so many times. She smiles up at her father, then releases his hand and races toward the cave entrance, all kit once more.

Vektal's expression is soft as he watches his daughter and then grows neutral as he looks to me again. "Ell-ee chose to stay with you?" His words are mild, but I know the question behind them —am I pushing her to stay because I want it, not because she wants it?

I feel a flare of irritation but push it aside. He is simply being chief. "It is true." I switch to sa-khui instead of the human English and tell my chief of Ell-ee and Erevair's appearances and Ell-ee's collapse. When his expression grows concerned, I explain to him her lack of eating and her strange mannerisms. How she will only eat after I have taken a bite. "Something has wounded her mind greatly in the past," I tell him.

He nods slowly, expression thoughtful. "Shorshie said she worried as much. They saw some terrible things when they were taken, and she says bad things might have been done to Ell-ee. That when the others take slaves, they do not treat them like people."

I frown at this. How else would they be treated? It is something I still do not understand. "Ell-ee is safe with me," I tell him. "I know she is slow to trust, and I want her to have as much time as she needs."

"Even with resonance?" my chief asks, arms crossing over his chest.

"Even so."

He studies me. "I believe you...and I am glad you are being reasonable."

I scowl at his words. "Why would I not be reasonable?"

"Why would I trust you to listen to reason after what you have done, Bek?" Vektal rubs a hand on his jaw and looks tired. "If you wanted a mate so badly, why did you not tell me of your plans? So we could work out the best possible way to handle it with the homeworlders?"

I clamp my jaw shut. I did not ask him because I knew he would say no. "I wanted a mate, and I did not care the consequences."

"Exactly. The moment a mate is a possibility, every male in my tribe loses their heads." He throws his hands up in the air. "What am I to do as your leader? Let you upset half the tribe with your actions? Do as you please even if it causes harm?"

"You were right to have the tribe shun me," I tell him. "Though I think it is a stupid punishment, you had to do something." I have had many days to think about this. If he had not exiled me, perhaps he would be chasing down Taushen, Harrec, Warrek and Vaza after they had stolen females. If there were no rules, none of the females were safe. "You did what you felt was necessary."

Vektal just stares at me. Then he moves forward and puts his hand on my brow.

I jerk away. "What are you doing?"

"Are you fevered? Where is this reasonable Bek coming from?" He tries to touch my brow again.

I slap at his hands. "He is about to stick a spear up your nethers."

He just grins at me, dropping his hands to his sides. "You did a good thing, retrieving Erevair. It almost makes up for your actions with the females. Almost. Have you decided to apologize yet?"

I still think demanding an apology is foolishness, but if it will make the tribe happy, I will do so just to quiet them. "Not yet," I tell him. At his surprised look, I add, "Not because I am unwilling, but because I wish to spend some time alone with my Ell-ee. Perhaps if we are away from the tribe a bit longer, she will learn to trust me."

Vektal nods slowly. "And perhaps resonance will be fulfilled?"

The idea seems so very far away from where we are right now. He does not realize how much of a gift it is simply to feel the touch of Ell-ee's hand. Mating with her seems as close as the stars themselves. "I am prepared to wait."

He claps a hand on my shoulder. "That is a good answer, my friend." He glances over and calls out, "Talie, come. We are leaving."

A moment later, Talie skips out of the cave, all bouncing curls and swishing furs. "I am ready, Papa!"

Vektal holds his hand out. "How is Ell-ee?"

Clever chief, to send his little daughter in so I cannot protest, and so Ell-ee will not be scared. “She is stinky,” Talie says cheerfully. “But I saw her smile.”

I am hit with a furious bolt of envy at that. Ell-ee smiled…and I was not there to see it.

Vektal nods again. “Good. Come, we will set some traps and see what we can catch, yes?” At her happy nod, Vektal raises a hand to me. “Return when you are ready, my friend.”

I nod, arms crossed over my chest as I watch my chief and his daughter leave. Then I turn back to the cave. Ell-ee is there waiting for me in the entryway, my spear in her hands.

And I am filled with pride and joy at the sight of her. I will get her smiles soon enough. I can be patient until then.

10

BEK

ONE WEEK LATER

"Eat," I tell Ell-ee. "You have only had three cakes this morning." I take a bite out of the cake in my hand—cake number four—and then hold it out to her.

She bares her teeth at me in a mock snarl, but takes the cake from me anyway and eats it with slow, reluctant bites, her look mutinous.

I just smile, pleased. Every chance I get, I push food into Ell-ee's hands. I make sure she eats several times a day, and I watch which meals she prefers to see what I should feed her next. It seems that my mate enjoys fresh meat—and unlike most humans, will eat it raw—and so we go hunting every day to ensure she has good food for her belly that night.

My mate still does not talk much, but she is becoming more relaxed with me. Now, when I push too much, she does not flinch. She lets me know her displeasure. She sleeps fitfully sometimes, but she has not tried to run, and she eats everything...as long as I take a bite out of it first. The hollow look is slowly fading from her eyes, and it seems to me that she is already putting on weight, which makes me happy. If she were as plump as Mah-dee, I would be greatly pleased. Mah-dee is very healthy and strong. Even as I think this, though, I do not care if she remains as small and fragile as she is, as long as she is healthy.

I am learning my mate's personality, too. She loves the outdoors. Snow does not deter her, nor does a sudden storm. If anything, I think she likes the bad weather more than the good. She loves a high breeze, she loves the sun on her face, and more than anything, she loves the stars at night. Sometimes she wanders out of the front of the cave and sits in the entryway just so she can gaze up at the stars. I join her, just to be at her side. To me, they are nothing but lights in the sky, but she can stare at them for hours.

Even more pleasing, my Ell-ee loves to go hunting. She is not good with a spear, but she loves to walk for hours and take the trails with me. She is patient, and her hands delicate, and she has learned to set some of the easier snares. I am proud of how clever she is, how willing to learn. I enjoy the company, too. She walks at my side tirelessly through the day, though at night she is quick to fall asleep, exhausted. She is smart when it comes to hunting, as well, staying out of the way when an animal flees, or handing me the right weapon when I must change tactics at a moment's notice.

We make a good team, if a quiet one. I do not even mind the quiet, either. The excited flush in her cheeks and her bright eyes when we take down a kill? That tells me everything.

Resonance is...difficult, however. With every day that passes, the urge to mate grows stronger and my lovely, delicate mate more difficult to resist. I still have not touched Ell-ee as I would like. Sometimes when she is having a bad dream, I will slip my hand into hers and she will cling to it until she falls back asleep. Other than the occasional brush of fingers, I have not touched her more.

I have not touched myself, either, and that is proving even more difficult.

As a hunter with no mate, I am used to taking myself in hand and giving my cock a quick tug until the worst of the tension is gone. But the cave we share is small, and Ell-ee skittish as a dvisti kit. I cannot imagine her expression if she were to wake up to find me with my hands shoved into my loincloth. Would she be aroused? Scared? I do not know, and I will not leave her side for longer than a moment, so I endure my cock's endless ache and tell myself that this is what I have dreamed of for so long. I have waited season upon season for a mate. Now that she is here, I can surely wait a few days longer.

My mind is willing, but my cock aches at the thought.

I watch Ell-ee to see if she feels the same gnawing ache that I do, but if she does, she makes no sign of it. Her hands never stray to her cunt or her teats, she does not watch me with hot eyes, and her sleep is regular when it is not interrupted by nightmares.

Patience, I remind myself. It has only been days.

But they are both the longest and shortest days I have ever endured, the most difficult and the most rewarding.

On this particular day, the weather is fine and so we are going hunting once more. The cache closest to the cave is full, but I have nothing else to do with my time save feed my mate and my tribe, so I am working on filling another cache. With everything we do, I explain it to my silent mate: why we freeze more kills than we bring home, why we scrape the hides, why we collect dvisti dung chips for fuel. She absorbs all of this information with a blink of her big eyes and a small nod to tell me she understands. And she picks up on things readily.

My Ell-ee is clever.

Because the cache is full, we have set our traps farther out from the valley itself, over the next rise. It means a long walk both coming and going, but I think Ell-ee enjoys it. She closes her eyes and turns her face up to the sunlight every chance she gets, and the beauty of her makes my cock surge.

It makes walking...difficult.

If Ell-ee notices my arousal, though, she says nothing. Her attention is completely focused on the world around us rather than me, and I am envious of the attention she gives a herd of dvisti in the distance, or the tracks of a quill-beast left in the snow. She enjoys everything, even the most menial of tasks. Hunting can be exciting, but much of the time it is walking familiar trails and checking traps. Often they are empty and must be set again, but Ell-ee enjoys this, too. She moves forward to each trap and resets them carefully and skillfully, glancing up at me for approval.

My mate learns fast. I nod approval, proud of her. She could do this by herself, I think, given a bit more time and confidence. But I would rather us do it together. She keeps me company, and I protect her. It works well.

Most of the traps we have set for this day are intended to catch hoppers. There is not much meat to each of the spindly-legged creatures, but my mate enjoys their taste, and so I will catch them for her.

One trap in particular is set near one of the hot streams that crisscross the snowy landscape like veins. Many of the animals we catch for food come near the waters to drink, and so it is a logical place for traps. However, it is clear that when we approach this one, our prey has gotten away. The snare itself—made of braided cord—has been dragged away to the water's edge, mud smeared all over the snow from the creature's fight with the trap's tight noose. Tracks are scattered everywhere, and there seems to be hot, thick mud on everything.

I grab one end of the cord and pull it free from the sludge, making a sound of disgust. I throw it back down again and wipe my hands. Not only is it covered in mud, but I am certain there is fresh dung in there as well. "Cleaning cord is not how I wanted to spend the rest of my day."

Ell-ee makes a small noise of acknowledgment and picks up the end of the cord, looping it around her arm, ignoring the mud that spreads up her leathers.

"Leave it," I tell her.

She ignores me, continuing to pick up the cord. "Just dirt," she tells me.

I want to tell her that the filth has ruined it, but I also do not wish to hurt her feelings in case she thinks it is a comment aimed at her. So I say nothing, watching as she steps into the mud to gather more cord. Her boots make a squishing noise on the banks, and she lifts the cord again, frowning as she realizes it is stuck on a bit of rock near the river bank. She knows not to go near the water because of the dangerous face-eaters, and I watch her give the cord a hard shake, and then a tug.

"Let me do it," I tell her, moving forward.

Ell-ee gives it another fierce tug. Before I can make it to her side, she loses her footing and falls on her back with a loud SPLAT.

"Ell-ee!" I shout, rushing to her side. I skid in the mud myself and flop onto the ground next to her in a mess of limbs. "Ugh." I lift my tail from the mire and let it flick back to the ground, beyond irritated.

My tail slaps at the mud and more dirt flicks onto my face.

Ell-ee raises up on her elbows, eyes wide. She looks at me. Blinks.

And laughs.

The sound is small and shy, as if she is reluctant to make such a noise out loud but cannot help herself.

It is the most beautiful thing I have ever heard. I stare at my Ell-ee in wonder. She giggles again and then flops back down into the mud, laughing. This is the first time I have seen her laugh, or smile, and I am entranced. A small chuckle escapes me. Her sheer joy is infectious. "You should have let me get the cord," I tell her.

Ell-ee gives another snorting little laugh and grabs a handful of mud, and then splats it right onto my nose.

I stare at her, shocked.

She recoils a little, her expression uncertain. As if she's somehow done something wrong and will be punished. Seeing that fear on her face makes my heart hurt, and I want to make it disappear forever. I lift my tail from the mud again and flick it in her direction. "You think that is funny?" I say, keeping my voice light and teasing.

Her face is covered in spatters a moment later and she gives a delighted little shriek. The tension is gone from her shoulders and she's laughing as she grabs another handful of mud and smashes it into my mane. I mock-growl and flick her again, then grab a handful of mud myself. I will never toss it on her, but I will play this game. I will just let her win.

The mud fight goes on for a few more handfuls, and then Ell-ee flops back down into the mud again, breathless. Her teeth are bright white on her muddy face and her mane is nothing but stringy filth plastered to her head. I love the sight of it. I do not care that she is covered in mud—and possibly dung—and layers of dirt from her past. If she let me, I would kiss her all over in this moment. "You are the most beautiful thing I have ever seen," I tell her, unable to resist smiling myself.

Ell-ee's laughter fades slowly, but her smile remains. "Too much dirt," she admits shyly after a moment, sitting up and wiping at her leather-covered arms. Her clothes are soaked with muck and sticking to her. She glances at the nearby stream and shudders at the sight of all of the thin, long tubes lining the shore. She knows as well as I do that a face-eater is on the end of each one.

"I have no soap-berries with me," I tell her. "We can melt snow and wash back at the cave." My mind fills with images of helping her bathe, running my wet hands along her soft skin and touching her all over. I have to bite back my groan of need, my khui singing an urgent song.

She bites her lip, considering. Her hands scrape along her muddy sleeves again.

"Are you afraid?" I ask, getting to my feet. I slip a little, my boots unable to find traction in the mud, but I manage to right myself and then offer her a hand up.

Ell-ee considers my hand. "Safe?" she asks after a moment.

I sense there is more to that question. Safe to take my hand? Safe to bathe? Is that why she never washes? Because it is safer in her eyes? Is her stink a form of protection? Armor?

My chest hurts at the thought. I nod at her. "Safe."

No matter how much my khui wants it, I will not touch her. She must want it first.

ELLY

A mud fight.

I'm still smiling over it, even if the clinging, smelly mud makes the walk back to the cave bitterly cold and uncomfortable. The warm mud cools right away, and by the time we make it back into the valley, my clothes are frozen and stiff and walking is difficult. My teeth chatter with cold until Bek suggests he carry me so I can put my hands inside his vest and share his warmth. I practically fling myself into his arms, shoving my hands under his clothing. In the last few days, I've gotten over my fear of Bek. He doesn't grab, or yell, and he's always very careful with me. I trust him, and I don't think twice about launching myself against him and letting him carry me.

My hands find his skin, and it's like I've found a personal space heater. God, he is warm. So very, very warm. I moan with relief and clutch at his hard, muscular abdomen, trying to leach his warmth into my own body.

I peek up at his face, and his teeth are gritted, his eyes little more than slits. "Sorry," I whisper, wondering if he's mad that I'm making him cold, or at the mud.

His mouth pulls down into a little frown as he glances down at me, and I stiffen. "You have mud on your nose," is all he says.

I wrinkle my nose, trying to free it without removing my hands from his warm body.

"I think you also have mud in your nose," he points out.

"Gonna have to stay," I tell him, and burrow down closer against his warmth, relieved he's not mad.

Bek chuckles and pulls me a little closer. "It can stay."

My teeth are chattering hard by the time we get to the cave, but then we're out of the wind and it's not so bad. Bek sets me gently on my feet and fixes the screen over the cave entrance, then makes a fire lickety-split. When it's blazing warmth, I move forward and put my hands out.

"Eh?" he says, sounding disapproving.

I freeze. "What?"

He just shakes his head at me and gets to his feet. He grabs the thickest fur off his sleeping pallet and holds it out to me. "You jump every time I speak. I will not hurt you, Ell-ee. Never."

I swallow hard and take the fur from him. "Sorry."

"Quit apologizing."

"Sorry."

He gives me an exasperated look. "I almost preferred your silence."

Is that so? I stick my tongue out at him.

Bek chuckles and points at me. "That is much better." He turns his back and waves a hand in the air. "Now strip. I will not turn around."

Strip? Out of my clothes?

"I can hear your teeth chattering still," Bek says with his back turned to me. "Strip and wrap the blanket around you. You will never get warm otherwise."

Oh. His words make sense. I drop the fur, tear off my frozen clothing, and then wrap the blanket around me. Immediately, the cave feels warmer, and I settle in near the fire. Long moments pass, and Bek remains standing with his back to me. I wonder what he is waiting for.

"Tell me when I can turn around," he says after another long silence. "I will not look at you naked, I promise."

Is that what he is worried about? I want to tell him that he is the only one that has ever bothered to clothe me. "Now."

He turns slowly and gives me a little nod of approval then moves to the fire. I watch him as he feeds more fuel to it, his big hands graceful and sure. For some reason, I am fascinated by his hands and the way they move. Maybe because they are enormous and strong, but he does not use them against me. At least, I correct myself, not since the sa-kohtsk hunt. Even then, he looked horrified at my bruises. I watch his hands move for a little longer and then tilt my head at him when he pauses, watching me.

"I liked your smile today," he tells me. "And your laugh. It was beautiful."

I say nothing, though I feel my face flushing with uncomfortable heat. They are words I like hearing, but I don't know what to say back to him. That I like his smile? His hands? That I like the way he is warm? They seem like terrible compliments.

Bek lifts his chin and gazes at my head. "Your hair is still mud and ice."

I touch a hand to it, and it's a hard, nasty mess. I wrinkle my nose.

"Do you want to wash?" he asks me. "I can get you water. I promise I will not look."

"Why?" I shrug at him.

"Why? Because...some of the humans do not like it. They are shy." His eyes narrow. "And you are shy. I thought..."

"Most owners do not give me clothes," I tell him.

"Owners?" He scowls. "I am not your owner."

I shrug. "You bought me. Who do I belong to if not you?"

"To yourself."

I make a little 'hmph' noise. It will take a while before I believe that one.

Bek frowns mightily at me then. "I do not understand why you are so focused on belonging to someone."

Me? Is he serious?

He cannot be serious.

I stare at him. It occurs to me that here, on this sheltered planet where people hand stuff over if you need it, that they have no concept of money. Or slaves, for that matter. Georgie and the others were on their way to be slaves, I'm told, but none of them have had to live as someone's thing. Someone's possession. For the first time since getting here, my fear gives way to anger.

Real, intense anger.

I pick up my muddy boot and throw it at his head.

He ducks it—as I knew he would—and the look of astonishment he gives me would be comical if I wasn't so angry. "Ell-ee! What do you do that for?"

"Do you even know what you've done?"

Bek looks as surprised at my bellow as I am. "What have I done?"

"You bought slaves! People!"

He squints at me. "I had you brought here."

"You bought us! There's a difference!" When it's clear he's not getting it, I grit my teeth and try again. "Okay. How do you think I got here, Bek?"

"Cap-tan and Trakan brought you."

Those must be the other two blue guys. The jerks that had the collar on my neck. "Where do you think they got me?"

His expression grows uneasy. "From..." He pauses, thinking. "Other aliens?"

"And do you think I went with them willingly?" Under the blankets, my fist clenches, in and out, in and out. I can't believe I'm spitting so many words at him. I can't believe I'm so mad.

I can't believe he doesn't get this.

He hesitates, and I see a flash of understanding on his face. "They stole you," he says after a moment. "I remember Shorshie saying this."

"Yes. Stolen. I was stolen when I was twelve. I've been a slave ever since."

He scowls again. "You are not a slave, Ell-ee."

I gesture at my boot. "Ask my shoe if it wants to be thrown in the fire."

Bek's jaw clenches, and he stares at the flames, not answering me.

"Ask it," I repeat firmly.

"You are not a boot—"

"Just ask it."

His nostrils flare, and he gives me an angry look and then glances down at my boot again. "It cannot answer, Ell-ee. It is a boot."

"That's right. It is a thing. It cannot decide. You own it, and so if you decide you want to take it and toss it into the fire, you can do that and no one will care. It's a thing." I gesture at myself. "Now, ask me if I want to be taken from Earth."

"Ell-ee—"

"Ask me if I want to leave my family and friends behind. Ask me if I want to go live in a cage where someone can feed me bad food or whip me or put a collar on me just because I am a thing. I am a thing that does not matter." I'm so angry I'm shaking. My entire body is quivering. I need him to understand this. To really, really get this. "Ask me if I wanted to come to this planet."

He recoils as if struck. His hand goes to his chest, rubbing the hard plate there. His khui is humming—mine is too—but the look on his face is nothing short of anguished. "You would not be here? With me?"

"I didn't have a choice, Bek. No one did. Not me, not Summer, not Gail, not Kate, not Brooke. None of us. We're given no choice, because to the people that stole us, we matter as little as that boot."

Bek stares at the boot in his lap and then back at me. His expression is nothing short of incredulous.

"You don't know what it's like," I whisper. "Every day, unsafe. Every day, scared. Every day, no control, nothing. Given from one owner to the next. You don't know what it is like." A hot tear slides down my cheek. Crap. I brush it away, because I don't want to cry. No one makes me cry.

"Then show me," Bek says quietly. "Show me what it is like."

11

BEK

Her tears hurt me. Normally it makes me feel frustrated and annoyed to see a female crying.

But my Ell-ee? My strong, brave Ell-ee? This...hurts.

My Ell-ee spits words at me, fast and furious, and it is clear she is angry. More than angry—bitterly upset. She needs me to understand this, and I am trying, but I cannot wrap my thoughts around the fact that a person would be treated so. That her wishes would be ignored. I thought Shorshie and the others...

And then I pause, because I have not given it much thought. They always seemed so happy, and I envied them and their mates. But I remember now, Salukh saying that Tee-fah-ni has bad dreams. And I remember Claire always weeping when the humans first arrived. I was impatient with her then, thinking she was weak.

But now I wonder. Was she hurting and afraid? And I did not understand and was cruel to her.

My stomach churns.

"Y-you want me to show you?" Ell-ee stutters. "What it is like to be a slave?"

I nod. "Show me. Make me understand."

She swallows, and it is clear from her expression that she is considering my words. "If you are my slave," she begins slowly, "you must do as I say. You are no more to me than this boot." She gestures at it again. "If you do not do as I say, you will get the shock collar."

There is no shock collar, but I understand what she is saying. I am to put myself in her position, to think of myself as if I were her, enslaved. I nod. I am ready. I want to see.

Ell-ee studies me. "Stand up. Take your clothes off. Slaves don't get clothes."

I hesitate. She is magnificent in her fury—even if my feelings are mixed at the moment—and my cock has stirred to life simply at the thought of undressing at her command.

"Shock collar," she says flatly.

"Eh? Give me a moment to think."

"You are a slave. You do not need to think. Now stand. Undress." Her words are cold.

I start to get angry, but I remember the pain in her eyes. I surge to my feet, frustrated, and begin to pull my clothing off. When my loincloth falls to the floor and I am naked, I stand straight. I do not want her to be afraid of my cock, or the fact that it is hard. I want to reassure her that I will never touch her unless she asks it.

But she only flicks her gaze over me, uninterested. "Make me tea."

Not a strange request. I move to the fire and set up the boiling pouch, then sprinkle leaves in, glancing at her as I do. She manages somehow to be filthy and beautiful at the same time, still caked in mud. I want to tell her to bathe, to let me feed her. But if she wants to do this first, then we will.

I wait for the water to steam, and then when the tea is ready, I pour it into my mother's cup and hold it out to her.

She doesn't even look at it. "Are there leaves inside?" At my nod, she continues. "Get them out with your fingers. Quickly. I don't want my tea to get cold." Her tone is imperious and unpleasant, and I realize she is mimicking how her owners talked to her. Is this what my fragile Ell-ee dealt with? Every day? For turns and turns of the seasons?

I...do not like it. The task is an easy one, but the way she treats me...

I stick a finger into the tea, then jerk it back out again quickly. Hot. "I am going to burn—"

"Yes," she says. "But I'm bored of this now. I would give you the shock collar and throw the tea aside."

I scowl at her words. "Ell-ee—"

"Over there," she decides, pointing at the entrance of the cave. "Go stand over there and put your back to me."

I cup the tea in my hands, frowning down at her. "For how long?"

"Shock collar," she says again. "And for as long as I want you to. You don't have a say in things. You are a boot."

This boot is getting angry. I put the tea down carefully and then storm to the front of the cave, my tail lashing. I duck out and stand in the entrance, planting my feet as I put my back to her.

It grows quiet.

I cross my arms over my chest as the moments pass, and I wait for her to say something, to continue with this foolish, irritating game. She is silent. Too silent. I let a few more moments pass before I glance back into the cave.

She is in her furs, lying down, her back to me.

My nostrils flare and my arms clench. This is not funny. This is ridiculous, to have me stand out here, naked, and to treat me like—

Like I am nothing.

It hits me so hard that I stagger, my knees going weak.

This is how my Ell-ee lived every day. She is showing me. She is showing me how much it hurt her, how scared she was. How helpless and out of control. No wonder she does not trust. No wonder she covers herself in dirt and does not speak to anyone.

I crouch low on my feet, my head hanging with shame. I bought her. I bought her and all the other humans like they were boots. Like they were nothing. They did not ask to come here. I realize now why Ell-ee burns with resentment. Why Chail and the others look at me with hard eyes. Why there is such disappointment in the faces of Claire, Shorshie, and the others.

I have made Ell-ee and the others...things. Things, not people. Things that do not matter.

My stomach churns again, and I vomit in the snow, sick.

I understand now. I understand, and I am sick at heart. I wanted a mate so badly I did not stop to think about what anyone else wanted. Ell-ee and the others came here, when they might have been taken home or taken to another place where they would be treated kindly. They were given no choice, just like they were given no choice when they were taken. It does not matter that my intentions were good, only that I have done the same thing to them that so many others have done.

I straighten, feeling tired and sad. I broke my mate's trust long before I even knew she was my mate. How can I ever expect her to forgive me? I turn to go inside, to face Ell-ee's anger.

Her back is still to me, her form small under the thick blankets, her mane a sticky, filthy mess clinging to her head. I watch her for a long moment, trying to think of what to say...and then I realize her shoulders are shaking. She is crying.

My spirit hurts. I move forward, back into the cave, and I kneel at her side. "Ell-ee. Do not cry, please."

She is silent, her body trembling with the force of her muffled sobs. "I don't want to go back. Ever. No cages."

"No cages," I agree. "You will never go back. I will die before I let anyone take you from my arms."

Ell-ee looks up at me, her eyes huge and shiny. "Safe?"

"Safe," I agree, meaning it with every bone in my body. No one will ever harm her as long as I am breathing. "Always."

She watches me for a long moment and then emerges from the blankets and puts her arms around my waist, pressing her cheek to my chest as she tries to control her weeping.

I am stunned. She wants me to touch her after all she has told me? After spitting angry words at me and showing me her hurt? I hesitate, then gently put my hands on her shoulders. Ell-ee burrows closer against my chest, and I hold her close, stroking her hair.

"Safe," I tell her, and I mean it.

I hold my mate for hours. Neither of us speaks, and Ell-ee cries quietly against my chest for a time as I stroke her back. It does not matter that we are both covered in mud and filth, or that I am naked, or that our khuis are resonating wildly. This moment is about comfort. I hold her close until her tears turn into soft hiccups, and then silence. And I touch her, because even as much as she hates strangers touching her, my touch seems to calm her. It is as if my hand on her skin reminds her that she is not alone, not a slave. So I keep my hands on her at all times, stroking her arm, or rubbing her back, caressing her cheek. I do not make it about mating. For me, it is all about comforting my Ell-ee and making her heartache ease.

"Can we go sit under the stars?" she whispers after a time. "I need to see them."

"Of course." I am reluctant to let her go, but when we detangle our limbs and stand, she keeps her hand on my arm, as if wanting to keep our connection.

I grab a blanket and then follow her outside. She does not go far, just a few steps out from the mouth of the cave, and looks up. A sigh of pleasure escapes her, and then she moves closer to me, her hands going back to my leathers and holding on.

I sit down and pull the blanket around my shoulders, then gesture for her to join me. I expect her to sit next to me, but she crawls into my lap and settles against me, and I cannot escape the surge of joy—and lust—I feel with her body pressing against mine. I wrap my arms around her, cocooning her in my warmth and the blanket, and she puts her head back on my shoulder and we gaze up at the skies. To me, they are just stars, but to her, they are something more, so I try to see them with her eyes. Is it the colors she enjoys? The immense yawning sky? What?

After a time, Ell-ee sighs, her gaze fixed on the stars above. "My first owner kept me in a cage for a long, long time."

I frown at this, wanting to ask questions but biting them back.

"He had a zoo," she whispers. "That's a place where you collect live animals and keep them to look at them."

She pauses, and I wonder if she is expecting a response. "It sounds...strange."

"I guess it is. It's not fun for the animals." Her fingers play along my arm, feeling the protective ridges of my plating. "The cages were much too small for most of them, and mine wasn't big enough for me to stand up. They never turned the lights off, and we were kept in this big enclosed area that was always a little too warm. It smelled like dung and piss and it was noisy." She shudders. "I hated it. I thought it was the worst thing possible until he got rid of his zoo and sold me to...someone else."

She grows quiet.

I stroke her arm. "What happened?"

Ell-ee exhales slowly. "My new owner was...mean. He liked to torture his humans. He liked to see our reactions."

I struggle to bite back my anger. "This is the one that fed you bad food?"

She nods. "Bad food, and that was just the beginning of it. Sometimes...I did not feel human at all." She goes silent again. "I don't like to think about it."

"Then say nothing." I hold her tighter. "I know you did not want to come here, but this place is safe. Cap-tan and Trakan says we are too far away from other worlds for most to visit. They tried to get us to go with them and said if we did not, we would never leave this planet again. We stayed, all of us. That means they are never coming back, and we do not have to worry about others. You are safe here. I promise this."

Ell-ee gazes up at the stars again. "You're sure?"

"I am certain." I remember how annoyed Trakan and Cap-tan were at having to return to give me the humans. I will never see them again. This I know in my heart.

She settles in against me. "I know the others think it's cold and ugly here, but...I like it. I like being outside so much. The stars are so pretty."

"We will come and spend time outside with the stars every night, if it pleases you."

"It does," she says softly, and I can almost hear her smile.

ELLY

I've never noticed my own filth much, because I can't really smell myself. But mud? It itches. By the time I wake up the next morning, my scalp feels dry and scratchy, my head heavy with the mud in my hair, and my skin crawls with the need to get clean. The thought of sliding my dirty body back into a set of new clean clothes makes me shudder.

I peek over at Bek. He's normally quick to bathe, but after our stormy fight last night, I notice he's still wearing traces of the same mud. He's still down to nothing but his loincloth, and I'm wearing my blanket and nothing else.

Funny how I'm not scared of him. I ranted and railed at him last night about my time as a slave, something I haven't been brave enough to do in...well, ever. Normally I'm utterly silent because silence can't get you into trouble. But last night, I said so many things that my heart hammered in my breast even though I couldn't stop myself. I was both terrified and angry at once, and when it was all done, just...drained.

But I feel better today. So much better. Cleansed. I shared some of what's been bottled up inside me for so long and I still feel safe. Maybe it's time for me to get rid of some of my dirt. I can't remember what it's like to be clean anymore.

I touch my hair and look over at Bek, uncertain. His hair is pretty, for a guy. It's long and thick and black, and he has a few braids woven in at certain spots to keep it out of his face. I study his features. He's not the handsomest of the aliens, I think. There's something a little too harsh and unforgiving about the curve of his mouth, and the hard line of his jaw. His shoulders are huge, and so are his hands. He doesn't look cuddly in the slightest. But...I like that. I like that he looks so mean. It means people won't mess with him. It makes him safer.

It's also weird that despite resonance, I don't feel like I'm trapped or bound to Bek. Instead, it feels like I have a friend. Someone I can trust. If I have to spend every day of the rest of my life here in this cave with him instead of in the village with the others...I'd be perfectly okay with that. I trust him like I trust no one else.

And I still get that hot, achy feeling between my thighs when he stands and turns his back to me, his butt flexing. I stare at it for a little longer than I should, fascinated by those bubbles of muscle above his thighs. He really does have a nice, firm butt for an alien—

He turns and catches me staring. "What is it?"

My mouth goes dry. My pulse is throbbing, and I can hear my cootie start up. "You have mud on your tail."

He grunts, accepting this. "I will wash soon enough."

"Can I come with you?"

"Of course. I would not leave you behind."

Oh, that wasn't quite what I meant. "Can I wash, too?"

He pauses, his gaze meeting mine. Then he gives me a quick, firm nod. "Of course. When do you wish to go?"

"Are we going to bathe...here? Or in a stream?" I know he normally bathes in a stream, but the thought of stepping into one with all those long-toothed fish makes me scared.

"Which do you prefer?"

"Here." I rub my arm and mentally wince when more dirt and mud showers off my skin. "I don't like the stream."

"Then we will do it here. We can check our traps later." He gets to his feet and moves to the fire, adding more fuel to it. "I will start heating water."

"Thank you," I murmur softly.

Bek pauses, tilting his head. "Do not thank me, Ell-ee. I am your mate. Anything you wish, I will make it happen for you.

There is no need to be thankful. It is my duty and one I am glad to do."

Okay then. I curl up near the fire and watch as he puts the pouch on and works on filling it with snow. He makes several trips to fill it, and then gets out a small pouch full of what look like berries and small pieces of worn leather. None of it looks like soap, and I touch my filthy hair again, wondering if that will even work on my layers of dirt.

He offers the pouch to me, and I take it, hesitant. "Is this soap?" I should have paid more attention back in the village. At his nod, I pour a few berries into my hand and sniff them.

"That is not how you do it," Bek tells me.

I blink up at him in surprise. "What?"

"Washing yourself. Rubbing them on your nose will not do much."

I stare at him. It isn't until his lips curve a bit at the corners that I realize he's teasing me. I laugh, because for a moment, I really thought he thought I didn't know how to wash myself. Which, given my appearance, wouldn't be out of the realm of possibility. "This really is your soap?" I ask, smiling.

"Yes. Shall I show you how to use it?" He fills a bowl with warm water, tosses in one of the leather rags to use as a towel, and then sets it down in front of me.

I can do it myself, of course. I'm sure I can figure out how to smash a few berries and make a lather of some kind. But there's a strange kind of appeal to the thought of him doing it, so I nod.

"Do you want to keep your blanket on?" he asks, moving to stand behind me.

It'll get wet, and I don't want to ruin a perfectly good blanket. I toss it aside and stand in front of him, waiting. I'm naked, but a naked body is nothing special.

At least, it's not to me. But as I watch, his jaw tenses a bit and his eyes flick over me before going to rest firmly on the bowl that he picks up. Is my nakedness bothering him, then? I watch him, curious. His cootie sings loud to mine, and I realize why he won't look at me. It's resonance. He's attracted to me, and my nakedness is making him think about...mating.

Funny how flushed that makes me feel.

Bek sets an old fur down on the floor at my feet. "To soak up the water," he tells me. "We will wash you from the mane down."

"Okay," I say softly, clasping my hands in front of my breasts so my arms stay out of his way.

"Close your eyes."

I do, and in the next moment, I feel warm water dribbling down my scalp, along with the wash-towel. He moves it over the muddy clumps of my hair, loosening the dried mud, and when it's damp, he tells me to hold still and begins to work the biggest lumps out of my hair. I remain still, keeping my eyes shut, and I pay attention to my senses. I can feel his warmth as he stands close to me, his chest bare. I smell a hint of leather and sweat when he moves, but it's a good smell. I like it. The rumble of his khui washes over me as his hands move through my hair, gently detangling, and every so often, his skin brushes against mine. It's like he's covered in velvet, and it feels good. I want to rub up against him...of course, I should probably wait to do that until I'm clean.

"I am crushing the berries to put in your hair," he tells me, voice soft. "It forms a lather that is good for cleaning, but your hair is so dirty it might need more than one washing. After that, I will comb it for you."

He will? Why do I like the sound of that? "Thank you."

Bek grunts. "Do not thank me. You are my mate. I do this because I enjoy it."

"So...no thanking, and no apologies."

"Correct."

I think for a moment and then squeeze one eye open. "Move faster, slowpoke."

He shoots me a look of astonishment, and then a slow grin spreads across his face. I'm smiling, too, because I can joke with someone for the first time in what feels like forever...and it's okay. Gosh, what a good feeling.

"Eyes closed unless you want soap in them," he commands, and I obey. A moment later, I smell the thick scent of something fruity, and then his hands begin to move through my hair again. His fingertips rub against my scalp, and I can feel the foam growing thick, sliding down my forehead. He swipes it away with a finger and goes back to massaging my head, and I want to moan with how good it feels.

I love this.

"Are you all right?" Bek asks. "Tell me if it is too much for you."

"Fine," I tell him shyly. My nipples are getting hard, and I want to cover them for some reason. He's seen me naked, but we're standing so close I don't want them to brush against his chest. Actually, I kind of do, but I don't know how that's going to make me feel. I get all shivery just thinking about it.

"Tilt your head back," he murmurs to me, so close that I can practically feel his breath on my skin. "I will rinse your hair, and then we will wash it again."

I do, and I feel the water splattering down my hair and my back. It's getting all over the floor, but Bek doesn't seem to care, so I don't either. My head feels lighter, and by the time he finishes washing my hair a second time, it smells fruity and clean. He gets more water and then takes the cloth and carefully wipes every inch of me with the soapy rag, going over my skin repeatedly to get it clean. I keep my eyes closed, just enjoying his touch and the rare sensation of someone caring for me. He goes over my face, my neck, my arms...but then he swipes the towel over my breasts, and my body breaks out in gooseflesh. I can't stop the gasp that escapes me, and I open my eyes.

Bek's intense gaze meets mine. "It is just to get clean," he says, voice hoarse. "I will never touch you without permission."

I nod, because I'm not sure what else to say. Is it bad that I want to rub up against him again?

Hours later, I'm so clean that I feel like a different person. I can't stop touching my soft skin, and sometimes I see my arm move and it's so pale I'm not even sure it's mine. Some of the worst snarls had to be cut out of my hair, and so we used Bek's knife to chop it to my shoulders, but the result is baby-fine, soft reddish-brown hair that I vaguely remember from my childhood. I like it. It feels so light and airy that I run my fingers through it, scarcely believing it's my own hair.

And Bek? Bek can't stop staring at me.

I notice it as I slip a clean tunic over my head and go to sit by the fire. He busies himself around me, mopping up the floor and tossing out dirty water, but every time he glances in my direction, he seems to stare for an extra long time, studying my face.

"What?" I finally ask, uncertain and shy. "What's wrong?"

"Nothing is wrong," he practically growls at me.

Nervous, I start to pull my hair over my face, to hide it.

"Do not," he says quietly. He moves to my side and squats down beside me. With gentle hands, he brushes my hair back from my face and tucks it behind my ears. "I did not mean to make you uncomfortable. I only stare because...you look different."

"Oh."

"I like it. Too much." His voice is gruff. "Never hide your face from me." Bek touches my cheek lightly and then gets to his feet. As he does, I notice a bulge in the front of his loincloth that he discreetly adjusts as he walks away.

Well. I don't know what to think of that.

No more is said as we sit by the fire and Bek repairs his weapons. The bone they use for their spears and knives wears down easily, he tells me, and must constantly be maintained. I offer to do it, but he just mock-growls at me, and so I sit by the fire and play with my hair a bit more. I just play with my clean hair and watch him work...and think.

I think a lot. Mostly about Bek. Namely...his body. After we finished my bath and I was wrapped in furs, my hair squeaky-clean, I was sleepy. I laid down to nap, and as I did, Bek heated water for himself and washed up. And even though I was supposed to be sleeping...I watched him. He washes himself in a much more brisk manner than he touched me. His hands slide quickly up and down strong blue calves, and I'm fascinated as the rag moves over his thick, muscular thighs. His tail flicks as he cleans himself, moving back and forth across that fascinating bubble butt of his. Then his hands move over his chest, and then...lower. I can't help but notice the large size of his cock and his, um, spur. I feel the pulsing between my thighs, feel myself grow slippery there, and I want to squirm.

I hated the way resonance made me feel at first. Now I'm both fascinated and terrified by it. I want Bek to touch me. I'm scared of what will happen if he does. I know how sex works—I've seen lots of slaves have sex with their masters, even if I never did—and it doesn't look pleasant. But I know it can be—should be. Georgie and the others wouldn't be so happy otherwise, or so quick to kiss their mates.

I touch my lips. Kissing. That's something else I've never done. Do I want to do it with Bek?

I think of his hard mouth curving at the corners to form a smile.

Yeah. I think I would like to kiss Bek.

I watch him as he works on a smaller knife, honing the edge of the blade to a razor-sharp edge. When he's satisfied with it, he gives it one more glance over and then flips it out to me, handle out. "What do you think?"

I take it from him, shy that he's asking my opinion. I don't know anything about knives. It looks fine, though. I run my finger along the edge, and it feels sharp. "Nice."

"It is for you," he tells me. "I will make you a spear, too, so we can hunt together."

It's for me? I hold it close to my breasts, ridiculously pleased. It's the nicest thing anyone's ever done for me. I open my mouth to say thank you, then close it again. He doesn't want thanks. So I just let my eyes show him how pleased I am.

He grunts, dusting the bone slivers off his lap, but he looks satisfied.

12

ELLY

Bek fills my thoughts for the rest of the night, and by the time I drift off to sleep, my mind is still on him. Instead of dreaming about cages and zoos and horrible things in my past, I dream about Bek. About blue skin and big hands that wash me with gentle care, taking extra time to caress my breasts with the soapy cloth. In my dream, I want him to go between my legs and touch me where I'm aching, but he never does. He just skirts around my thighs, rubbing my belly with the cloth over and over again until I make a sound of protest.

I wake up, a whimper in my throat, my hands between my thighs. I'm wet and aching, and I feel so needy. My nipples hurt, and all of me feels restless. My hand between my legs feels good, though, and I can't resist stroking my fingers up and down my folds. It feels too intense to do more than that, though, so I caress myself a few times, careful to keep away from the more sensitive areas.

"Ell-ee?"

Bek's husky voice makes me freeze. I look over at him in the dim light of the cave. The fire's not more than a few flickers amidst the dung chips, and I can only see a vague shadow where Bek is, except for the bright glow of his eyes in the darkness.

"You were moaning in your sleep," he tells me, concern in his voice. I hear the furs rustle as he gets to his feet. "Was it a bad dream?"

Oh no. It wasn't a bad dream in the slightest. In fact, it was the opposite of a bad dream. If he wasn't talking, I could actually go back to the dream. "It's nothing," I say quickly, and squeeze my thighs tight around my hands. I don't want to remove my hands from there. I want to keep touching myself because it feels too good to stop.

"Are you scared?" He drops down to crouch next to my bed. "Do you want to hold my hand while you sleep?"

In the past few days, when I've had bad dreams, he's let me hold on to him and it helped. Right now, though, he can't hold my hand...because it's between my thighs and sticky with my arousal. I should say something. Tell him to go away. To let me sleep.

Instead, I do nothing. I let him peel the covers back, and he sees my hands pressed at the junction of my thighs. He groans, khui humming, and I bite back a whimper of my own.

"Are you touching yourself, my Ell-ee?" His voice is so low and husky that it feels like a caress.

I nod, biting my lip, and stroke my folds again while he's watching. It feels deliciously naughty and bold all at once. I want him to see it, though. I want to know what he's going to do, how he's going to react...and if he likes it.

The breath hisses from his lungs. "You want me to watch?"

I do, I think. I rub myself again, squirming on the blankets, and then stop, because I keep touching spots that feel far too intense.

"Why do you stop?" he asks, settling down onto the blankets next to me. He's not touching me, not yet, and I want that desperately. His touch is safe. His touch makes me feel comforted. Not alone. "Ell-ee?" he asks when I remain silent.

"I don't know," I whisper. "I've never done this."

"Never?"

I shake my head. I never had the privacy before. Never wanted to. Never looked at a man with fascination over the play of his muscles like I have with Bek... I feel different around him. Alive.

And I want his touch. I remember the way it felt to have his hands on me as he washed me, the velvet softness of his warm skin, the feeling of his big body next to mine. I moan and stroke myself again and then stop.

"Are you afraid?"

"A little," I admit. Whenever I touch myself while thinking of him, things feel so intense. I stop because I'm afraid of that intensity. It makes me anxious.

"Can I join you under your furs?" he asks.

My heart hammers in my breast, even as my cootie's song grows louder and louder. "Yes."

Bek slides under the blankets next to me, and his leg brushes mine. He pulls me close, tucking me against his shoulder, and it feels weird considering I still have my hands between my thighs. He's still wearing his loincloth, and I can feel the leather against my skin—and the hard erection trapped underneath it. But he doesn't do anything other than settle my body against his. "Now you can keep touching yourself," he tells me. "I have you."

He does, and I feel the small knot of anxiety go away. But I want more than just this. "I want you to do it," I tell him, my voice small.

There is a long pause, and I feel his body tense next to mine. "You...wish me to touch you?"

"If you want to."

He caresses my jaw, the small touch enough to make my nipples ache. "My mate, nothing would bring me greater joy. But I do not wish to frighten you with touches you do not want."

And that's why I want him. Because he's careful with me. Because he's safe. So I take the hand that's tracing my face and guide it lower. My breath quickens, because I'm both terrified of this and excited by this.

"Your fingers are wet," he murmurs, letting me lead him. "Is it because you are wet?"

A small whimper escapes me, the only answer I can give, and I slide his big hand to my breast.

"Do you wish me to touch your nipples?" he asks. "Or shall I just stroke your skin?"

I want it all. "Yes."

He chuckles low. "That does not answer my question."

"Both."

"I can do both," he tells me. His fingers lightly skim over my skin, caressing, and I feel the calluses on his hand rasp against my skin. It's a mixture of scratchy and soft, hard and warm, and I love it. I love the way his big hand cups my small breast, and he makes me feel so protected against him. I burrow my face against his neck and inhale his scent. I want to wallow in all of him.

His fingertips graze over my nipples, and I moan, because it sends a jolt straight to my insides. My cootie thrums in my breast, and his is singing as loud as mine. It feels as if my entire chest is vibrating with its excitement, and it's turning me on, too.

"My brave, sweet mate," Bek murmurs against my hair, and his thumb rubs over my nipple. "You are the most beautiful female I have ever seen."

"Because...yours?" I pant, arching against that delicate touch. It's the most teasing, frustrating, delicious thing I've ever felt.

"Even if you were not mine, I would think you beautiful." His nose rubs against my cheek, his breath warm against my skin. "Soft, small, strong and so lovely."

I moan at his words, because I like the thought of him finding me attractive despite our resonance.

"I like your pale skin," he whispers into my ear, his tongue flicking against my earlobe. His hand slows, and then he gives my breast another caress. "I like your small teats with their pink tips." He strokes my belly and then brushes his fingers over the curls of my sex. "And I like this little tuft here."

"You do?" I've noticed the sa-khui are hairless there, and I wondered what he would think.

"I do," he tells me, and his tongue drags against my earlobe again, making me shudder. "Because it hides your folds. It teases me with what could be underneath." He strokes his fingers over the curls again. "Do you want me to touch you and find out?"

I give a sharp little cry and cling to his muscular arm. I want it more than anything else in the world right now.

"Tell me," he whispers, and nips at my ear.

"Yes," I pant, nearly beside myself with the aching need of all of this. "I want that."

His big fingers skim lower, and then he's finally, finally touching me. It's just as intense as I imagined. His big finger rubs against my curls and then glides downward. He traces the seam of my folds, leaving me gasping and clutching at his forearm. That's all he does, though—just rubs. "More?" he murmurs into my ear.

I give him a quick, jerky little nod.

"My brave mate," he tells me, and then dips his finger deeper. It glides through my slippery folds and traces up and down, learning my most sensitive parts. I moan and squirm, holding on to his arm and panting. He brushes his finger over my clit and then goes lower, pressing deep against my core before dragging back up and playing with my clit again.

It feels like too much. Like I'm going to explode. I can't handle it, and I push his hand away, gasping.

"What is it?" he asks, nuzzling my hair again. "Tell me."

I shake my head, unable to articulate it. "Feels like there's something wrong."

"Wrong?"

"Makes me shaky when you touch me there. Like...something's going to burst."

His eyes narrow at me, and he rests his hand on my belly. "Ellee...have you never touched yourself? Made yourself come?"

I shake my head. "I lived in a cage. No privacy."

"Your parents did not teach you about mating?"

"I was taken when I was young. I...don't remember us ever talking about it." I let my fingers play on his arm. I love touching his arm, because it's so powerful. "I know what mating is, though. I've seen others do it to their slaves."

"Did they ever pleasure their females?"

"No. Why would they?"

"Right. Slaves." He looks thoughtful, then presses his mouth to my forehead. "Does it scare you when I touch you? Because of how you feel?"

"A little," I admit. My khui is going wild, my pulse throbbing. It almost feels like I'm going to explode if he touches me there again.

"It is nothing to be afraid of," Bek says softly. "You touch yourself until you cannot bear it any longer, and then your body..." He pauses, thinking. "It goes a bit further, and everything inside you feels as if it is shouting with joy. It is an intense release."

"I like the touches," I admit. I'm just not sure I'm ready for 'intense release' or my body shouting. Already I miss his hand between my thighs, though, and I wiggle against his palm, hoping he'll touch me again. Just...not too much.

"Do you want me to show you what it is like?" he asks. "To stroke yourself until you come?"

BEK

Her lips part with surprise at my suggestion. There's a lovely flush over her pink skin, and I want to press my mouth to every exposed bit of skin and lick it. I want to bury my face between her thighs and mate my tongue to her cunt. I want to do so many things to her. But if what Ell-ee says is true, she does not know how to touch herself properly.

I do not want to scare her with my mating enthusiasm. I want her to enjoy herself. I want to see her come, to see her eyes close and the expression of bliss on her face when she gets her release.

I watch as she nibbles on her lip, and I want to lean in and taste it, to mouth-mate with her as the other humans do. I was never fond of it with Claire, but with Ell-ee, I think it will be different. So many things already are. "You would show me?" She buries her face against my shoulder, clearly embarrassed. "I feel silly."

"Why?"

"Because this is something I should know...isn't it?"

"Just because you have never had the chance to touch yourself does not make you silly." I fight back my helpless anger at her captors. At the people who stole her as a child and kept her in a cage. My mate, in a cage. Like an animal. If I think about it for too long, my mind will go black with rage and I will lose control of my anger. I cannot change Ell-ee's past, but I will make sure her future is perfect. "I can show you, and then we can make sure you come, as well." I touch her cheek, because I cannot help myself. I want to touch her all the time. "There is nothing to be embarrassed of."

"All right," she says shyly and gives me a curious look.

I debate getting to my feet and standing in front of her, but I like the feel of her body curled up against my side, the feel of her skin brushing against mine. "Can I kiss you first? A mouth-mating?"

Her gaze flies to my mouth, and then she looks at me again and nods, shy.

I put my hand in her shiny, clean mane and pull her closer to me. Our mouths are close to touching when I admit, "I might not be very good at this."

She giggles. "Me either."

I love her laughter. It sounds so bright and happy. If I can make her smile, surely I can give her pleasure. I lean forward and brush my mouth against hers in the gentlest of caresses. She holds still, not moving, and I wonder what she thinks. I pull back and study her. "Bad?"

She touches her mouth. "I don't think so. Have you never done this, either?"

"I have. I had a pleasure-mate several seasons ago."

"Oh." My sweet Ell-ee looks downcast at that.

In this moment, I regret every caress I ever gave another. I should have waited for my mate. "There was no love between us," I tell her, stroking her cheek. "She left me because she thought I was mean, and soon after resonated to another."

Ell-ee looks startled. "Mean?" Her hand goes to my chest, and her fingers rub small circles against my plates. "Really?"

"Really. I was not patient with her. Not kind. I regret that."

She studies me. "You are always kind to me."

"It is different with you. Everything is different with you."

"I am glad." She lays her head on my shoulder again, and her mouth curves into a little smile. "It is the same with me. I have not felt like anyone was safe before you."

"Even if I brought you here?"

"Even if," she agrees. Her fingers move to my jaw, and she touches me in a light caress, her fingertips stroking over my skin. "I have you, and I have the stars. I'm safe. I don't need more than that."

I groan, wanting to bury myself inside her sweetness. This small female has my heart in her hands. I want to give her so much pleasure...but I will start with my own, so she knows it is nothing to worry over. I press my mouth to hers again and let my tongue graze over the seam of her lips. She gasps, and when I pause, she presses her mouth to mine again. It's a silent request for more, and I am happy to do so for my mate. Our lips meet again, and I deepen the kiss, allowing my tongue to slide against hers. Her little whimper of pleasure makes my cock ache like never before.

Kissing Claire was never like this. It felt uncomfortable, as if I was doing something wrong. But with Ell-ee, it becomes a sensual pleasure. I lick at her mouth, letting my tongue mate with her as my cock wishes to. Over and over, our mouths meld in a tangle of wet kisses, lips and tongue, and I am lost to the sensation. Her hand curls against my chest, and she brushes her teats against me as she knots her hands in my hair, deepening the kisses.

By the time I pull away to catch my breath, I am panting. My mate looks dazed, her mouth pink, wet and swollen from my caresses. She's crawled into my lap as we've kissed, her legs straddling my aching cock. And she no longer looks scared, just rosy with desire.

The sight of her is so enticing I want to fling her to the floor and push into her, but I must go slow. I must show her what it is like. "I must take my loincloth off," I tell her, my voice thick with need.

"Oh." She looks confused for a moment, as if just now realizing that she is sprawled in my lap. After a moment's thought, she moves down my thighs and sits on my knees. "Is this okay?"

Gazing at my naked mate as she straddles my legs? Enjoying the sight of her breasts and spread thighs as I stroke my cock? "Fine."

Her hands rest on my thighs, and she gives me an expectant look, waiting.

I undo the laces on the sides of my loincloth, then tug the leather aside, revealing my erect cock and spur to her. She looks curious but not worried, studying me with a tilt of her head. Then she looks up and meets my eyes.

"Does it feel soft like me?" she asks.

I groan, because now I am thinking of the soft, wet feel of her cunt against my fingers. My khui is singing loudly, so strong that my chest feels as if it is shaking, and when I reach down to grip my cock, I can feel the pre-cum slicking down my skin. "Hard," I tell her thickly.

"Can I feel?"

Was ever a male so tortured? I nod, holding my breath.

Ell-ee puts her hand on me, encircling my cock with her fingers —or at least, trying to. They cannot go all the way around my shaft, and her hand looks small and pale in comparison to my thick length. She lets her hand move up and down in a light caress. "Hard and soft at the same time," she tells me. "Your skin is soft, but underneath…like rock."

I am going to burst. I close my eyes and try to think of anything other than the mind-blowing pleasure of my mate touching my cock. I think about cages, instead, and that sobers me enough to regain my control. Ell-ee's fingers trace the ridges going up the length of my shaft, and then she circles the head, letting her fingers play in the thick, wet pre-cum there. Since I have resonated, my seed has grown thicker, less clear, and I know it is so I can put a kit in my mate's belly.

She finally withdraws her exploring hand and gives me a shy look. "I would say thank you, but—"

I growl at her.

She giggles, and it is the sweetest thing I have ever heard. I grip my cock again and give it a hard stroke, pumping from the base of the shaft to the head. Her laughter turns into a gasp, and she gives me a fascinated look. I love that my mate is staring so intently at my cock, and I stroke it again for her. Over and over, I stroke my aching cock. I have used my hand to pleasure myself many times in the past, so I know how to do it quickly, and the resonance is making my need greater than ever. I want to last for a long time to show off for my mate, but it will not happen this time. Not with her straddling me, her face so close, her expression so focused and full of concentration. I continue to work my cock, flicking my wrist when I reach the head and tightening my grip as I do. I want to tell her all the things I imagine doing to her as I stroke it—picturing her teats rubbing up against my shaft, or her mouth dipping low to tongue the head. Or watching from above as I feed my length into the hot well of her cunt. Turning her over and spilling my seed down the pink curves of her bottom. All of these things ripple through my mind, but I keep them silent. There will be time for that later. For now, I perform for my mate.

My breath hisses between my teeth, and I feel myself close to coming. I deliberately slow my movements, drawing it out, and when she leans in, it becomes too great to resist. "Back away or I will spray your face, my mate."

She looks startled and leans back. I fight back a surge of disappointment—there will be other days to paint her mouth with my seed—and work my cock harder. My strokes are rougher, more ragged, and I can feel my sac tightening. I graze my other hand over my spur, and then I come with a low growl, my seed shooting into the air and splattering on my stomach and thighs. Ell-ee gasps, and I continue to work my cock with hard strokes, working every bit of seed out of my body until I am finally spent. I pant, trying to catch my breath, and watch my mate.

Ell-ee's lips are parted, and she looks fascinated. "Did that feel good?"

I nod, but it would feel better if I was deep inside her, her walls clenched tight around my cock. "It will feel good for you, too," I tell her thickly.

She licks her lips and gives me an uncertain look. "I don't know." Her hands slide between her thighs and she strokes herself then bites her lip again. "I want you to do it, I think." She gives a little wriggle on my knees, and I see her nipples are erect, her skin prickled with bumps.

It would give me great pleasure. I grab my loincloth and use it to clean myself up, then toss it aside. She immediately crawls back into my arms, her teats brushing against my skin in a deliberate manner. Even though I just came, my cock responds to her nearness. I ignore it, settling her against me until she is comfortable. She puts her arms around my neck and tilts her face up for a kiss, and I need no further urging to claim her mouth.

As our mouths mate, I put my hand on her side and let it slide down to her hip. She moans against my tongue, pressing her teats against me again. "Tell me you wish me to touch you, Ell-ee."

She presses a tiny kiss to my mouth and nods, her eyes shining as bright as the stars she loves.

I let my hand slide to the inside of her thigh and then stroke her folds. She's wetter than before, so slick and juicy that it makes my mouth water. Her fingers tighten on my neck as I stroke her, and she moans. I avoid her sensitive little third nipple at first, because it makes her nervous. I want her to come, though. I just need her to want it as badly as I do. So I continue to pet her, caressing her slippery folds and teasing the entrance to her core. My mouth claims hers in another fierce kiss, and our tongues continue to lock as I rub a finger against her core and slowly push it in. She whimpers, and I go still, but then she kisses me harder and rocks her hips, and I know she's mine. When my finger is seated deep inside her warmth, I begin to stroke it slowly, like I want to use my cock.

I press light kisses to her mouth and let her ride my hand, making my thrusts gentle and slow. She has never mated before, and her cunt is tight; I do not wish to harm her. I want her to enjoy this. Her noises become more urgent, her movements jerky. Her nails dig into my skin, as if she is desperate to hold on to me.

"I have you," I murmur, and slide my thumb through her folds, seeking the little nipple nestled there.

Ell-ee cries out when I brush my thumb pad over it and buries her face against my neck. She clings to my arms, but she is not pushing me away, and so I continue to stroke her, loving every shudder and every little noise she makes. She whimpers, her hips moving faster, and then I feel her bite at my skin, her blunt teeth doing their best to dig into my shoulder.

I groan, because it is one of the most erotic things I have ever experienced. "My mate. My sweet mate. I have you." And I stroke her nipple again.

She bites harder, making choked little sounds as she clutches my arm. "Bek," she cries out when I let my thumb drift over it again. "I can't—"

"I have you," I tell her firmly. "Let it happen."

Ell-ee makes a sound that's half-cry, half-groan, and then I feel a hot rush of liquid between her thighs, soaking my hand as she comes. She holds on to me, panting against my neck, her khui thrumming furiously in time with mine.

"You did well, my mate," I tell her, and stroke her hair with my free hand. "Are you all right?"

"I...ooh." She slides off my hand and tumbles back into the furs, lying on her back. There's a completely dazed expression on her face.

"That is what happens when you come," I tell her smugly, and cannot resist licking her taste off of my hand. No drop of this should be wasted.

She watches me with a little shudder, her hands moving back between her thighs and she cups herself.

"What are you thinking?" I ask her, curious.

"That I should have done that years ago," she says, a dreamy expression on her face.

My bark of laughter echoes loud in the cave.

13

ELLY

The next week that follows is the best week of my life.

I love being with Bek. I love our quiet little life out in the cave together. Our days take on a routine, and instead of it being boring or dull, I find it comforting. I love that I know what to look forward to with each and every day.

We no longer sleep apart. After that night of making each other come, I crawled into his furs and we kissed and petted each other until we both came, and then we went to sleep. I held his hand as I slept, and my nightmares didn't come. After that, we decided we needed only one bed in the cave.

Our routine is a good one, too. I'm a light sleeper, so I wake Bek up each morning before dawn with kisses and caresses. Now that it feels safe to touch him, I'm addicted to the feel of his hands on my skin. I think I grope him far more often than he gropes me. I know he's trying to be careful and not scare me, but I know in my heart that he's safe now. I know he would never hurt me, and so I constantly look for ways we can touch or fool around. And there are many of them.

After our morning cuddle, Bek insists on feeding me. He carefully takes a bite of my food before handing it over for me to eat, and sips my tea before I drink it. I trust the food now because it comes from him, but I'm touched that he goes out of his way to make me comfortable. It's like I don't have to change who I am to please him—he's perfectly fine with accommodating my quirks, and I adore that.

Once we eat, we go out and watch the suns rise, hand in hand. It's one of my favorite moments in a day that's already full of good things, but I love to see the suns peek out over the purple mountains. Once the suns are up, we get our weapons and check our traps, or go hunting for the day. I enjoy fresh meat, and I love it raw, strangely enough. More than anything, I just like that I have my two favorite things—Bek and the outdoors—all day. I'm not very good with a spear, but my trap-work gets better by the day, and I hope to be able to pull my weight, given time. Sometimes we collect roots, but most hunted kills go toward one of the ice-caches that are so important for the brutal season—or so Bek tells me.

When the suns start to go down, we return to the cave with our dinner. We make a fire, eat, and then move to the front of the cave to watch the stars come out. After it gets too cold to stay outside much longer, we move inside and under the furs.

I...might be addicted to masturbating.

Maybe it's the cootie, or maybe I'm making up for lost time, but I love touching myself and having Bek touch me. I have a one-track mind, and as soon as I hear his cootie begin to hum for whatever reason, I want to drop everything and have him shove his hands down my pants. I've tackled him while hunting, during breakfast, and during bathing. I've flung my arms around his neck and kissed him until we're both rubbing each other wildly. There's no rhyme or reason to it—the moment I want Bek, I go for it, and he's always willing to give me more.

We don't do more than touch each other, though. I touch him, he touches me, and we both always come, but we haven't done more than that. We haven't had sex, and so resonance is still unfulfilled. I haven't minded that, because I love the touches we've been sharing.

But I wonder if my cootie is getting impatient, because it seems to be extra horny today, and even pausing twice to make out on the trails today hasn't satisfied it.

In the evening, I sit by the fire. It's not yet time to look at the stars, so I'm sharpening my knife like Bek showed me, and my girl parts ache with need. My cootie hums low and urgent, and no amount of squirming in my seat is making it better. I glance over at my alien, and he's got his head down, working busily to plait a length of leather rope for one of the traps. His mouth is pulled into a frown, and he looks so irritated at the menial task that it makes me all hot and bothered. So grumpy. I know what will make him smile.

I put my knife aside and think dirty thoughts, and my cootie goes from a low hum to a fierce, urgent one. Bek's khui answers the call, and he looks up in surprise as I approach. His mouth curls up on one side, and he puts aside his cordage. "Now?"

"Now," I agree, stripping off my leather tunic and sliding into his arms.

He chuckles, pulling me against him until I'm straddling his crossed legs and his cock is resting right against my most sensitive parts. "You grow insatiable, my mate."

I shrug. I don't care as long as we're both happy. I slide my hands down his chest, then push his vest open, exposing his pectorals. He's fascinatingly hard here, not only with muscle but with the strange, thick plates that grow over his skin in certain spots. They always make me want to bite him, and today is no different. I put a hand on the back of his neck and lean in, letting my mouth drift over his neck in a soft caress before I nip him.

I love the groan he makes. I rock my hips against his cock, encouraged. "Let's go do this out in front of the stars." I love being outdoors. Stars and my Bek together? Sounds perfect.

"The fire might die—"

"Then you will keep me warm," I tell him, and rub my hand up and down his length. I'm not going to take no for an answer... but I know it won't be no. It's never no.

He grins and gives me a kiss, then pulls me off his lap so he can get to his feet. I eagerly jump to mine, ready for another round of kisses and caresses. Bek pulls me against him a moment later, his hands on my breasts. "You have a ferocious khui, my mate. It—"

"Ho," calls a distant voice from outside the cave.

Bek's expression changes from playful to startled, and he immediately grabs a fur from the floor and tugs it around my naked upper half. He grabs a second fur and pulls it around his waist, hiding his erection. "Come in, Rokan."

I slide behind him, all of my excitement disappearing. Everyone in the tribe is nice, but they're not...safe. Not like my

Bek. I don't know them like I know him, and I sure don't trust them. I hover behind my mate, and I can feel myself shrinking in, the words locking in my throat.

As if he senses my unease, he puts an arm behind him, and I cling to it for reassurance. Touching him makes me feel better.

A moment later, a tall hunter strides into the cave. He's wearing a fur cloak tossed over his shoulders and a pack on his back. He raises a hand in greeting, his smile easy. "Bek, my friend." He peers behind him and smiles at me. "And Ell-ee, though I scarce recognize you. Did I interrupt something?"

"Yes," Bek says. He sounds grumpy. I'm a little grumpy, too, because my cootie's gone silent, and the wonderful throbbing feeling between my thighs has disappeared.

Rokan just laughs. "Never change, my friend."

Bek grunts.

I stare at Rokan, ignoring his smile. I hunch my shoulders, and I want to tilt my head forward to let my hair hide my face...but my hair is no longer stiff with dirt. It's soft and smooth and shorter, and it doesn't do much for hiding.

"So you are talking to me now?" Bek says to Rokan. "Or does your shunning need work?"

Rokan only grins, not put off by Bek's unpleasant tone. "Would you prefer that I shun you?"

"I would prefer that you leave." At Rokan's surprised look, he continues. "I am not sure my Ell-ee is ready to be around others just yet."

He can tell that? I feel a stab of guilt, sliding my hand into his. I don't want him to choose between his friends and me, just because I'm not good with people. But Bek grips my fingers tightly and gives them a squeeze. He's letting me know it's okay. That he's got me.

And I feel a little bit better at that. As long as he's at my side, I can adjust to living in the village with so many strangers. Maybe I'll even be able to talk to them. Maybe.

Rokan moves toward the fire, ignoring the fact that both of us are wrapped in blankets. He crouches near it and warms his hands, rubbing them. "It has been a long run out on the trails, my friend. Sit. I will not stay long."

Bek sits again, the tightness in his jaw easing a bit. He looks up at me and gestures that I should sit, too.

I feel safest when his arms are around me, so I immediately drop into his lap and pull his blanket tight around both of us. Bek tucks my head against his shoulder and gestures at the fire. "There is tea on, if you wish some, Rokan."

Rokan only watches us with amusement, flexing his hands. "I am not thirsty. Like I said, I will not stay for long. I am too close to home, and I long to see my mate and our son." His expression grows soft with pleasure. "It has been far too many days since I have seen her."

"Did you have good hunting, then?" Bek's hand strokes my arm, reassuring me, and I relax a little more.

"Some, but I did not accomplish what I needed to. I am returning early. There will be a fierce snowstorm soon. I wanted to warn the tribe."

"Bah. There is always snow."

Rokan shakes his head. "No, this is a great snow. One that will rival the brutal season. It will not be safe for humans to be out in the cold. I must make sure that Raahosh and Leezh are not out hunting, or Mah-dee with Hassen. I sense it will be a very cold storm for a long while." He glances at me. "And I suspect our chief will want you to bring your mate into the village so she is safe."

I expect Bek to blow off his words, to make a dismissive sound and ignore him. But he is quiet, his hand stroking my arm thoughtfully. Then he nods. "I will make sure she is in the village. How long do we have?"

"A handful of days. When the moons disappear from the sky, I think. I can see the storms in my mind's eye, and it will be a big one. Far too much snow." He straightens, hands on his hips, stretching. "And now that you have been warned, I am going to continue on to the village. I saw the smoke from your fire in the distance and thought I would warn you."

"It is night out. Do you want to stay for the evening? You still have a few hours of travel to go." Bek gestures at our cave. "We have room, and we have food."

"No," Rokan says. He straightens his cloak. "The weather is pleasant yet, and being in my mate's arms is even more pleasant." He turns to the cave entrance and gives us a small wave. "I will see you both in the village soon."

"Mmm." Bek raises a hand in goodbye.

I say nothing, a little puzzled by the sudden appearance—and just as sudden exit—of Rokan. "Is it dangerous for him to go?"

"Rokan? No. He can sense things we cannot. And he is never wrong about a storm." Bek presses a kiss to my brow, thoughtful. "If he thinks it is not safe for you to be out here, I must take you back to the village."

I slide my arms around his waist, pressing my cheek to his shoulder and enjoying his warmth. "I don't want to go."

"I know. I would keep you here with me if it was safe, but I cannot risk you. You are the most important thing in my world."

His words are confusing me. He makes it sound like he won't go back with me, but Vektal told him it was fine. "So when will we return?"

"We will gather enough food to make sure you are well supplied for the storm, and then we will head in. Perhaps two days."

He's avoiding the question. "And you're going with me?"

He is silent.

I push against his chest, frowning. "Bek? You wouldn't leave me alone in the village, would you? I don't want to go back without you!"

"Ell-ee," he says, voice ragged. The look on his face is troubled. "It is...difficult."

"It shouldn't be! They're your people!"

But his expression is bleak and fills me with worry.

BEK

Ell-ee is upset at me. I can tell by the stiff way her shoulders are set. She climbs out of my lap and moves to her furs, her delicate jaw set in a stubborn angle. She does not want to go back to the village by herself.

And I do not want her to go. Not at all. My greatest joy is having her at my side, hearing her laugh, seeing her face. Every day is better when I wake up with her at my side and go to sleep with her hands on my chest. It does not matter to me that we have not mated yet and my body aches with need for her. I want her to feel comfortable and secure. I want her to look forward to it with joy. More than anything, I want her to tell me she is ready. I do not want to push her.

I do not want her to go.

But...I am not sure I should go back to the village with her.

Vektal has given me permission. I am sure that if I return, some will look at me with glad eyes. My sister will be pleased. But I do not know that Claire will forgive me. Or the other humans. I remember Shorshie's helpless anger when I did not understand why she was upset. And I think of the four new humans that were recently brought here because of me. They hate me.

They all hate me. And how can they not? I bought them. I did not realize how bad a thing this was until my Ell-ee explained it to me. Until she showed me what it is like to not matter to someone who controls your life. I realize it now, and I am sick at heart at what I have done. In my eyes, I was saving the humans. In their eyes, I am no better than those that stole them.

So I do not know if I can go back. Not yet. Not until angry tempers have cooled.

But I also do not know if I can leave my sweet Ell-ee's side. I do not want to abandon her...but I also do not want my tribe to hate me more. What if the other unmated males are full of resentment that I have brought females here for them and yet I am the only one with a mate?

There are so many questions in my mind, and I do not know if they have answers. I look over at my mate. She sits in her furs, her shoulders slumped, the happiness in her eyes such a short time ago dulled. It hurts me to see this. I have done this to her. I have made her sad. "Ell-ee, talk to me."

She shrugs. "You're going to abandon me." Her expression is stiff, but there's a wobble in her voice. "You think I want to go back there? I want to stay here with you."

I want that, too, more than anything. I move over to her side and sit down next to her in the furs, cross-legged. I do not touch her, but my knee brushes against her pink one. "I do not wish to leave your side—"

"Then don't," she replies quickly. "Don't abandon me."

"I did a terrible thing," I tell her. "I bought humans because we wanted mates. The others are still angry at me, and I do not wish for them to hate me more."

"Vektal said you could come back," she tells me again. "He's the chief, right? So they have to go by what he says."

She is right, and yet… "If my presence makes the others unhappy, I will have no choice but to leave again."

"Then I'm going to go with you," she cries, wrapping her arms around my waist. "We go together, wherever we go."

I pull her close, burying my fingers in her soft mane. I want that more than anything. "You would give up a tribe just to be with me? You would give up home?"

Ell-ee leans back and gazes up at me, her eyes shiny. "Bek, I never had a home before I got here. I was never safe. You are my home. You are my safe. I'm with you forever."

My heart feels impossibly full. I cup my mate's upturned face and kiss her mouth gently. "Even if I am a bad male who bought people?"

"You didn't know what you did," she says simply. Her hands touch mine. "And once you realized, you were sorry. There's a difference between that and those that will never look at slaves as people. Who use shock collars. Who torture slaves just to be cruel. You could never be cruel." Her expression grows thoughtful. "Though I do remember one time when you knocked me to the ground and covered me with bruises at a sa-kohtsk hunt..."

I am full of remorse and shame. "I thought you were running away. To leave at that moment would have been death. Ell-ee—"

"I'm teasing," she says lightly, and takes my hand and kisses the palm. "I love you, Bek. Even when you're impatient and grumpy."

"Not with you. Never with you."

Her smile is brighter than the stars. "Never with me."

"You are my world, my mate." I study her beloved face, humbled that I am lucky enough to resonate to such a female. "I wanted a mate, but I never imagined one as perfect as you. I am lucky beyond my wildest dreams."

She slides closer, her hands going to my thighs. "I never knew what it meant to be happy before I met you, Bek. I thought I would be miserable here because it would just be another place I'm trapped. But with you, I don't feel trapped. I feel safe. Like I have someone to belong to. Like I have something to look forward to every day."

There is a knot in my throat. I wrap my arms around my Ell-ee and crush her against my chest. My mate. My everything. No male has ever been so lucky.

And then when I feel her little tongue slide along the side of my neck, I chuckle. My cock immediately aches. "Even now, you wish for me to pleasure you? My female is insatiable."

"You've created a monster," she agrees, tracing one finger along the arch of my horn.

"I wish to please my monster," I tell her, and imagine laying her down on the furs, my mouth between her thighs. I want nothing more than this. Nothing.

"Then put your hands on me."

"I would put my mouth on you, Ell-ee." I lay her gently in the furs and then pull her leggings off. She is already half-naked, my mate, but I have her completely naked in a matter of moments. "I would kiss your cunt and lick you until you cry out."

She gasps and gives a little wriggle on the furs, titillated by the idea. "You would?"

I groan. My fearless mate. "It would give me great pleasure. You do not know how much."

Ell-ee's hands go to her thighs. "Then I get to do the same to you once I've come."

Ah, my lovely mate. "Very fair." I lean in and press a kiss to the inside of her knee, then the soft inside of her thigh. Her body trembles as I move up, the scent of her driving me mad. My mouth is watering at the thought of being able to taste her. There is a saying that nothing tastes better than being between the thighs of your resonance mate. I have been waiting many days for this, and my khui sings an urgent song of agreement.

I kiss up her thigh, and she gives a little shiver as I pause and then spread her thighs wider so I can feast upon her. Her pink folds are exposed to my view, wet with need, and I cannot resist giving her a long, slow lick. The strangled moan she gives makes my cock pulse with need. I want more. I part her folds and bury my face in her sweetness.

Ell-ee cries out, arching, and I anchor an arm around her hip, holding her steady so I can lick her. Already, I am addicted to her taste. I need to have this every day, need to wake up with the taste of her on my lips. After days and days of touching, I know which caresses she likes best, and I use my tongue to give her those. I trace little circles around her third nipple and swipe my tongue over her sensitive flesh in long, languid strokes until she's rocking against my face, her breath rapid little pants of excitement. Her hands are fluttering over my mane, my horns, as if she wants to hold on but does not wish to bother me. As if I would stop until she cries out. I drag my tongue over her sweetness and lap at her core, then push the tip of my tongue inside her.

This time, she locks on to my horns and moans loudly. Her skin prickles with bumps, and a fresh wave of juices coats my tongue, a sure sign that my mate is already about to come. Pleased at how quickly I can bring her to pleasure, I lick my way back up to her third nipple and tease it until she makes that gasping, choked little sound that tells me she's almost there. I do not stop, tonguing her over and over again.

She comes with a stiffening of her body and a little shriek, and I lick up her release, loving the taste of her on my mouth. My mate. Mine.

Nothing—no one—will ever part us, I decide. If the tribe does not want me, we will leave. We will make our own tribe if we must.

I just want my Ell-ee to be happy. If she is happy, I do not care where I am.

14

BEK

We stay out in our small cave for two more days before we load up the sled with food supplies and begin the walk back to the village. Ell-ee insists on carrying a pack, though I would gladly take her burdens for her. My mate has a fierce spirit, but she is still thinner than I would like. The sled is full of fresh animal meat and roots we have harvested in our walks in the last few days, so we do not return to the tribe empty-handed. It is an easy walk back to the village—no more than a few hours—but as we journey, I notice that Ell-ee moves closer and closer to me until she is practically holding on to my belt by the time we make it to the pulley.

She is nervous. Afraid. I want to ask her why she is afraid, after all this time. After living with the sa-khui for several days before coming to stay with me, but I know the answer. She is happy with me in the cave and feels safe.

And she does not trust that to continue.

It makes me ache to think that she is so full of fear. My people are good people. I know that given time, her fears will go away, but until then, she will worry. I must do whatever I can to make her feel safe, then. We pause so she can rest, and each time, I hold her close and kiss her to distract her. Perhaps it is not very restful to encourage our khuis, but if she is thinking about mating, maybe she will not worry about rejoining the tribe so much.

"All will be well," I reassure her as we approach the pulley that will let us down in the gorge that houses the stone village. Her cold fingers are wrapped tight around the leather of my belt, and her face has taken on a pinched look of concern.

"I just don't want us to be separated," Ell-ee tells me. "If they won't let you come back, I don't want to come back, either. I want to go with you. It doesn't matter where."

I want to reassure her that we will not be separated, but I remain silent. Resonance mates have been separated in the past when one needed to be punished. I remember Raahosh's brief exile, and Hassan's as well. I do not want that to happen. I do not want to leave my Ell-ee's side for a moment.

I look over at my mate, and her round face is somber and pale, and she looks at the pulley as if she is facing down her worst nightmares. "It will be all right," I reassure her. "We will still go watch the stars every night and watch the sunrise every morning."

"Even in the village?" She looks skeptical. "It doesn't get much light. Tiffany has to constantly move her trees all day to catch the sunlight."

"We can come here and ride the pulley up to watch the suns rise every morning," I tell her. I am happy to wake up a little earlier if it means so much to her. "And I will cut a hole in the roof so you can watch the stars every night until you fall asleep."

Her mouth curves in the faintest of smiles. "It's not a very good roof if it has a hole in it."

I put an arm around her shoulders and hug her slight form to me. "I will make sure you have them, one way or another."

She smiles, then, and presses her face against my chest. "I love you," she whispers.

My spirit swells with affection. "You are my heart, Ell-ee."

It takes time to load and secure the sled onto the pulley, and both Ell-ee and I ride down with it. Once at the bottom, I begin to undo the straps while Ell-ee waits patiently.

"Ho! Who is that I see before me?" calls a familiar voice.

I straighten, and Ell-ee automatically moves to stand behind me. Harrec. I raise a hand to him in greeting, pleased to see my friend. "You are just in time to help us with the sled."

"Am I?" He smirks at me. "I am a busy hunter today—I must go catch seven fang-fish before the suns go down."

It seems an odd thing. "Why?"

Harrec shrugs. "Because Kate thinks I cannot, and I must prove her wrong." He grins and then moves forward to help me haul the sled off the platform. "Is that Ell-ee I see behind you?"

I wait for her to greet him, but she is silent, her hands knotted into the back of my vest. "It is. Rokan says there is a bad storm coming in soon."

"Ah yes, his great storm." Harrec gives me a mischievous look. "I think it is an excuse so he can stay home with his pretty mate and rub her swollen feet."

"Bah." As if Rokan would lie. His mate is with kit for a second time, but he knows his duty as a hunter. "Careful he does not hear your words or he will rub your face into the snow."

Harrec just laughs and then slaps the side of the sled. "Well, come on. Pull this thing, lazy one. I have a pretty human I wish to prove wrong."

"Are you sharing Kate's furs? Pleasure-mating?" I ask as we haul the sled forward. There is not much snow at the bottom of the gorge, and it makes pulling far more difficult.

"That one? She would slit my throat before sharing her furs with me." But he looks rather pleased at the thought. "I am going to wear her down, though. Wait and see."

Harrec can indeed wear a person's nerves. He likes to talk, and more than that, he likes to hear himself talk. "Any resonances while we were gone?"

"Not a one. I think Taushen is despairing of ever getting a mate."

I grunt, hauling the sled forward as Harrec pushes. My Ell-ee moves quietly to the side, standing in the shadows of the cliff walls, out of the way. I give her a little nod to reassure her and let her know this will not take long. "And Warrek?"

"That one is so quiet, who knows what he is thinking." Harrec shrugs.

"Maybe it is not that he is quiet, but that your mouth is just open all the time," I tell him, and then grunt when the sled finally lodges into familiar ruts in the ground. "There it is. My thanks for your help."

Harrec just grins and rubs his hands eagerly. "I hope you are in the mood for fang-fish tonight, because I am about to prove to Kate that she has underestimated me."

"Luck to you," I tell him with a snort, and then look over at my Ell-ee. I pat the front of the sled. "Come sit, my mate. I will pull you in."

She moves forward, quick to put her hands on my arm and reassure herself. I pull her in for a kiss to her brow.

"You look different, Ell-ee," Harrec calls as he steps onto the pulley. "Resonance agrees with you." The look he gives us is sly and full of teasing.

I growl at him, and he quickens his pace, hauling the pulley up with speed and laughing as he disappears. "Ignore that fool," I tell her. "He speaks just to hear his own boasting."

She settles in at the front of the sled and then gives me a little smile. "Some people like to hear their own voice."

I grunt. That is one way Ell-ee and I are perfectly matched. We are both content with silence. I press another kiss to her—this time to her pink, soft mouth—before we set off. The walk to the village once you are in the gorge is a brief one, and soon enough, I can hear the laughter of the kits playing in the village, and the scent of smoke carries on the wind. I am hit with a wave of longing. These are my people. My tribe. I love them. If they will not accept me back, or let me be with my mate, I will have no choice but to leave. But I will miss them.

"Are you okay?" Ell-ee asks, her voice soft. It's as if she can sense my thoughts. "You look tense."

I turn to smile at her. "I wish for this day to be a good one, that is all."

"It will be," she says confidently. "Of course they're going to want you back. You're a badass."

I am not quite sure what that is, but she makes it sound good. "It is up to the chief, but I hope you are right."

"I know I am."

We round the corner of the canyon, and there is the village ahead of us. People are out and about, standing in front of their huts or talking near one of the central fires. A few of the kits are playing foot-ball at the edge of the village and rush out to meet us. Pacy and Kae race around the sled, giggling, and are joined by Raashel and Talie. "Bek! Where have you been?" Raashel demands, as bossy as her mother. "You haven't been here to play foot-ball with us."

"I have been hunting," I tell her, and ruffle her mane as I go past, hauling my sled. "Are your parents here?"

She nods. "Papa and Mama are talking to the chief."

So they are in the village. That is good. One less thing for the chief to worry about. "That is where we are headed." I pause to grab the foot-ball before it bounces in front of the sled and toss it away. They go chasing after it, full of laughter. I watch them go, my heart bursting with pride—someday my kit will be there, playing with them.

I glance back at Ell-ee, and she gives me a shy smile. She looks uncertain.

I know what will make her pleased. "Which hut would you like, my mate?" I stop the sled and gesture at the rows of uninhabited huts. There are many with no roofs, more than enough for twice the number of families that are currently in our village.

Her eyes widen, a silent question in her gaze.

I nod. "Since we are mated, we get to have our own hut, to raise our family. Chail will have to find herself a new person to share her hut with." Though if I know Vaza, he has already moved in, provided Chail is even the slightest bit willing.

My mate considers the rows of huts and then points at one on the far end of the village, at the outskirts. She wants to be away from everyone. Somehow I knew that. I grin and pull the sled in that direction, then set it down in front. "It is a fine choice, my mate, and will give us plenty of opportunity to get away for star-watching."

Her smile widens.

I help her down off the sled, and she begins to undo the straps. I glance around, and I can see others heading in this direction, and I know soon enough we will be swarmed. People will be wanting to greet Ell-ee and wanting to gossip about us. They will want to know about our resonance, and my shunning. Before anything, though, we must speak to my chief and see where we stand. I take Ell-ee's hand and pull her away from the sled. "Come. Let us go speak to Vektal before anything else."

She nods and moves to stand close to me, her other hand sliding to my belt.

I pull her through the curious onlookers, toward the hut that belongs to Vektal and Shorshie. As we move toward it, I see others are gathered in front, and I scowl, imagining they are all here to come stare at my Ell-ee. But a moment later, Dagesh steps out of the chief's hut, his mate next to him, and both of them are all smiles.

"Bek! You are back just in time to celebrate with us, my friend. My No-rah and I have resonated once more!" His look of delight dies a moment later, and he claps a hand over his mouth. "Oh, wait. Should we be shunning you?"

Before I can reply, Vektal emerges from the hut's doorway, his gaze focusing on myself and Ell-ee.

"My chief," I say, though my heart pounds in my chest. "I wish to speak to you."

He looks to Ell-ee, then to me, and gestures at his hut. "Come inside."

I put a hand on my mate's back, leading her inside. The chief's hut is much the same as any other, for all that he is chief. There is a fire in the fire pit, furs lining the edges of the hut, and a scatter of clothing and toys on one side that are evidence that his girls were playing nearby. "Where is your mate?" I ask him, pulling a stool near the fire for my Ell-ee.

"She went to get Claire the moment she heard you were in the village. I was on my way to greet you when Dagesh and No-rah came to see me with their news." His smile broadens. "Our tribe is growing."

I nod. "I am happy for them." I want to bring up the subject of my shunning, but it seems like an odd switch of conversation. I hesitate.

Ell-ee slips her hand in mine, giving my fingers a squeeze. Reassuring me. I am not worthy to have such a wonderful mate. My khui thrums a loud agreement.

Vektal sees us join hands and crosses his arms over his chest, cocking his head. "I see you are getting along. Have you fulfilled your resonance?"

"Not yet. We are taking things...slow." I gaze down at my mate, and she puts her cheek on my hand, content to remain silent. "Ell-ee has had a difficult past, and I do not wish to rush her."

There is no response, and I glance over at my chief. He has a look of pure astonishment on his face. "Bek?" he says, surprised. "Bek does not wish to push someone into doing something? Bek?"

I scowl at him. Ell-ee's fingers tighten on my hand as if she, too, is scowling.

Vektal just gives a shake of his head. "I am surprised, that is all. It is a good thing, trust me. Take as much time as you need. As long as you are happy, Ell-ee, I am content."

Before I can respond, the flap over the door is pushed aside and Shorshie and Claire enter. "Oh good," Shorshie says with a smile. "You're here."

I nod. "I—"

Claire sweeps forward and grabs me in a hug, her arms going around my neck. I am so startled by this, I remain perfectly still, not knowing what to do. Ell-ee's fingers squeeze mine tightly, even as I awkwardly pat Claire's back with my free hand.

"Thank you," Claire says against my neck, and she sounds weepy. She releases me a moment later, wiping at her eyes. "Thank you for rescuing my little Erevair. I nearly lost my mind that day—"

Oh. So much has happened since then with my Ell-ee that I had forgotten about this. "Your son has an adventuring spirit," I say, uncomfortable with her tears. Always tears with her. Claire is a good friend, but I have never known what to say when she weeps...which is often around me.

She gives me a punch in the arm, half-laughing, half-crying. "You dick. It's because he wants to be like you. Next time you hang out with him, try extolling the virtues of staying at home."

"He wishes to be like me?" I am filled with pride and wonder. "Is it because..." I struggle to think of a word, then remember Ell-ee's. "I am bat ass?"

Shorshie smothers a laugh behind her hand, while Claire just gives me a strange look. "What?"

I turn to Ell-ee. "Bat ask? Do I say it wrong?"

She moves closer to me. "Badass," she whispers, her face serious. Ell-ee would never laugh at me. With me, yes. Not at me. I know it is hard for her to speak in front of others, and she is brave to do so. I smile at her and touch her cheek.

"Badass," I confirm with the others. "That is what I am."

Claire giggles. "And so modest, too."

I nod thoughtfully. "If you think so, yes."

She throws her hands up in the air and gives a shake of her head, then comes forward to hug me again. "I wanted to say thank you, you big lug. Thank you for keeping my son safe." She gives me a squeeze with her skinny arms and then turns to Ell-ee. "I'm sorry to be all over your man. I'm just grateful to him, and I know he's going to make your kits a wonderful father. I'm happy to see he's finally found someone." She beams at my mate. "And I hope we can become friends."

Ell-ee stares at her for a long, long moment. Then, slowly, she gives her a tiny, almost imperceptible nod.

It is enough for Claire. She smiles at both of us and clasps her hands. "Come find me here when you're done and we can talk. Erevair would like to say hello, too." She smiles at Ell-ee again. "And I'm sure I have some stuff for your hut so you guys can set up house." She gives us all another little smile and then nods at Shorshie. "Okay, I'm going now."

Shorshie moves to Vektal's side and links her arm in his. "We're glad to see you both back. We were a little worried when Rokan mentioned the storm. Said it was going to be a bitterly cold one."

I remain quiet for a moment, then give Vektal an uneasy look. Ell-ee squeezes my hand again, then rubs her other hand on my arm, silently encouraging me. I suck in a breath and say the words. "I was not sure I would be welcome."

Shorshie looks to Vektal, waiting for him to speak.

Vektal puts a fist over his heart. "I told you how I felt. You have saved Erevair. It is enough for me if you wish to come back."

I shake my head, because it is not enough. It does not excuse what I did. "Being with Ell-ee has taught me many things," I tell them. "I did not understand at first that what I did was so terrible. My heart was in a good place, but Ell-ee showed me what it is like when someone is a slave. She made me realize that even though I meant well, I still did a bad thing." I release my mate's hand and drop to my knee in front of my chief. "And I want to say that I am sorry. To you, and to the humans I brought here against their will."

The room is silent.

"Wow," Shorshie says after a long moment. "I was not expecting that."

Vektal puts a hand on my shoulder. "To your feet, my friend." When I rise, he puts his other hand on my shoulder and gives me a proud look. "All I wanted was for you to truly understand. To realize the consequences of your actions when you force others to do as you please." He gives me a half-smile. "It sounds like Ell-ee has been good for you."

"Bek has been good for me," Ell-ee says quietly, surprising all of us. I turn, and she moves to my side, her hands going to my arm. Her face is pale but determined, and I know she is struggling with her shyness. "He has been nothing but kind and gentle to me. I know we were hard on him at first, but I am happy here, and if it weren't for him, I'd still be a slave." She looks up at me, her heart in her eyes. "He is a good man."

I feel intense pride and joy. Not only that my chief and his mate have accepted my apology, but that my mate stood up for me but defended me, even though I wronged her. I am humbled by the way she sees me...

And I vow I will do my best to be worthy.

ELLY

"Oh, girl, these people can't sing for shit," Gail breathes, clapping her hands to the awkward drumbeat. "What the hell?"

I just quietly chuckle from my spot at the edge of the group near the fire. She's right. There's a song—I think—that the elders are singing, and it's painfully bad. They're extremely enthusiastic, though. Off to one side, Vaza beats a drum with enthusiasm if not much skill, and someone passes around a skin of some smelly fermented drink.

There's a party going on tonight. It's not only in honor of Nora and Dagesh—he of the tongue-tangling name—and their second resonance, but of Bek's return to the village. Mine, too, though I'm not much of a celebrator. I prefer to stay in the corner with Gail at my side and watch everyone have a good time.

Bek is off by the fire, his gaze flicking back to me as if he wants to watch over me even when he can't be at my side. He's been dragged off by one hunter or another, and I'm proud of my mate. I'm proud he's such an integral part of this tribe that they're all clearly happy to see him again and to have him back. He's taken each new human member of the tribe—Gail, Summer, Brooke and Kate—aside and quietly apologized to them, and maybe it's the sincerity in his voice or the warmth and friendliness of the village, but no one seems to be holding a grudge.

I've been greeted and exclaimed over by so many people that I'm dizzy with the attention. It doesn't matter that I've been here with the others since Bek brought us—clean, well-fed Elly is apparently a big deal. It makes me feel good, if slightly uncomfortable, and I'm happy when Bek shoos everyone away so I can go sit in a quiet corner with Gail.

At my side, Gail laughs aloud, clapping her hands again. She leans in toward me. "Look at that fool," she says affectionately, nodding at Vaza. Her new 'boyfriend'—or pleasure-mate, as these people call it—is banging his drum with what can only be described as 'sexy' enthusiasm. At least, I'm pretty sure he thinks it's sexy. It just looks downright awkward to me. "He's lucky he's got a good heart, because damn, he tries harder than any man I have ever met in my life." She gives a little shake of her head. "I'm not sure if he thinks he's gonna score tonight with that drumming or if I have to look forward to some other form of flirting to come."

"More singing?" I tease shyly.

"Lord, no!" she laughs, and raises her hands in the air. "Heaven help me if the man comes and serenades me."

I smile widely, because I love Gail. I love her no-nonsense affection. It's clear she adores the attention that Vaza showers on her, and they seem happy together. She misses Earth sometimes, she says, but this feels like a fresh start to her, and she's willing to embrace it.

Me too.

"Elly! Elly! Look what I've got!" Erevair runs over to me again and drops into my lap. "Papa made me a new ball! Isn't it something?" He holds the hard leather ball up to my nose, nearly knocking it into my face.

I nod at him encouragingly.

This is apparently a sign for Erevair to tell me the story of his last ball and all the many adventures it went on before he lost it. Erevair is an incredibly chatty child, and he's picked me to be his audience, it seems. Every time I sit down, he drops into my lap and begins to talk my ear off. I think it's because he adores Bek, and by proxy adores me as I'm Bek's. It's kind of cute, and I don't mind—if I'm listening to a story, I don't really have to contribute much. I still feel tongue tied around these people. They're so happy. So peaceful. I gaze around the fire, at Nora and Dagesh, who are the happy center of attention. At Rokan, who's stroking his mate's slightly rounded pregnant belly. At Maddie and Hassen, who are making out by the fire as if it's their resonance night. At the cluster of children sitting in front of Sevvah and Kemli, listening to a story. At the hunter who walks past, a sleepy baby cradled in his arms so his mate can keep chatting with a friend. They're just a big family. I don't quite fit in. Not yet, but someday, maybe.

I'm content to wait. As long as they let me go at my own pace, I'm happy.

"And then the ball went under a bush! A greaaaat big bush this big." Erevair flings his little arms out. "And I went to look for it and couldn't find it. I looked and looked and it wasn't there! And—"

I nod, pretending to pay attention even as I glance over at Bek. He's speaking to Stacy, and as I watch, he grabs a little bowl from her with a nod of thanks and then heads to my side. He's so handsome, his steps fluid and strong, his blue skin shadowed with firelight, his horns proud. I give a happy little sigh, and my cootie starts singing rather loudly.

"Elly, are you listening to me?" Erevair puts a little hand on my cheek, startling me. The touch makes my skin prickle, but I realize a moment later it's just a child, and I calm down again. He's looking at me with a frustrated little pout.

I nod at him brightly, trying to reassure him.

It works. The story of the ball continues. "And then I went to get Papa because my ball was gone. It was just gone! And then—"

"Erevair," Bek says, dropping to a knee beside me and Gail on our skin. "Can you go show Harrec your ball? I bet he has not seen it yet."

"He hasn't?" Erevair climbs out of my lap, hugs Bek's arm, and then races through the crowd over to where Harrec is sitting, no doubt near poor Kate. He caught eight fang-fish this day and has not stopped bragging about it to her. I've seen many eye-rolls in his direction tonight, but I can't say she's hating his attention. Maybe it's just me, but I could swear I catch her smiling.

Bek settles in next to me. "Erevair is a handful," he admits, then shows me the bowl of not-potato cakes he's gotten from Stacy. "Food," he says, and picks up a cake, takes a bite, and then offers it to me. "Eat."

I smile at him and take the cake, eating it with small, careful bites as he tastes the next one. So thoughtful. I worried that things would change between us when we got back to the village, but Bek is the same as he's always been—careful and attentive to me, and protective. When others try to come talk, he puts his arm around me and pulls me close, answering for me when I don't respond. He wants me to be comfortable.

I love that. I love him.

I eat all of the cakes he passes my way, and Gail gets up to go 'enjoy' more of Vaza's music—or maybe to ask him to stop. I put my head on Bek's shoulder and sigh.

"Tired?" he asks.

It does feel like it's been a long day. I'm not...quite tired, though. I feel both wired and exhausted at once. There are so many people here that I just want to get away, but...I also want to spend more time with Bek.

He leans in, brushing my hair back behind my ear, and whispers in my ear. "Want to go look at the stars? Alone?"

"More than anything," I whisper.

He gets to his feet and offers me his hand, and I take it. By the fire, Kate and Summer are talking about some TV show, their voices high-pitched with excitement, and the group roars with laughter at something. I pay no attention. My hand is in Bek's, and we're going to look at the stars.

15

ELLY

We lay out blankets in our new hut and lie back, gazing up at the stars. We have no roof yet. Bek tells me that he will work with Hemalo tomorrow to ensure it is put on very soon. A privacy screen hangs in front of our door, and even though our house is open at the top, we're alone and no one will bother us. Tonight the weather is clear, though, so we are merely a little chilly. I press closer to Bek under the blankets, stealing his warmth. From the bottom of the gorge, there's not much sky available, but there's a sliver along the edge of the cliffs that shows me enough stars to keep me happy. I know they're there, and that's enough.

I play with Bek's fingers as we cuddle, thoughtful. For all that my mate is not as smiley or full of laughter as some of the other men in the tribe, it's clear that he's loved. He's a good person and a hard worker. I think of all the children that came up to him over the course of the day, wanting to say hello, or to play, and how he gave them all attention as if they were just as important as any adult. For some reason, I've not given much thought to children, but of course there will be kids. Resonance means babies.

And Bek and I resonated. That means we should have babies. But...so far we haven't had actual sex. If you'd have asked me when I first landed here if I wanted to have sex with Bek, I'd have been appalled at the thought. In the past, sex has always meant a lack of choices, of dominance over the partner, of something a girl is forced into. But so much has changed between then and now. I trust Bek...and I love it when he touches me.

He doesn't want to rush me, but I'm not scared. Given time, I think I can get used to the village, and I love being here in the outdoors.

More than anything, I love being with Bek.

My mate nuzzles my hair. "You are thoughtful."

"Because I'm quiet? I'm always quiet."

"Because you normally gaze up at the stars and make happy little sighs." He presses his mouth to my hair again. "Tonight you just toy with my fingers. What is it you think about?"

He knows me well. "The tribe."

His body tenses a little against mine. "Are you unhappy?"

"I'm happy." I think about Gail and how happy she seems. She likes Vaza and likes the attention he gives her, and she loves children. There are tons of children in the tribe, and someone is always needing an extra hand. Summer and Kate have become good friends and seem to be blending in well with the tribe, and at the big gathering, Brooke had been surrounded by the little girls of the tribe who wanted their hair braided.

Everyone seems to be finding their place, even if it's something as small as braiding hair. Even though we didn't choose to come here, this is a much better place than we were in. "I'm glad the other girls seem to be adjusting well." I would feel weird if I was the only happy one and the others were miserable.

Bek grunts acknowledgment. "No other resonances, though."

"Maybe they're on birth control. Maybe they're like Gail and can't have more children." I stroke his chest, letting my hand trail down the muscular lines of his flat stomach. "It doesn't matter as long as they're happy."

"Mm. I would like others to have a chance to resonate, though. It does not feel right for me to have everything I want and for them to wait."

"You can't control everything," I tell him, amused at the thought. My Bek wants families for his friends as fiercely as he wants one for himself. That's sweet. "Though I like hearing you have everything you want."

He hugs me closer, and I can hear his khui purring. "Is it not obvious?"

I sit up, gazing down at him. "You want children, though, don't you? So you don't have everything yet."

Bek strokes a hand down my arm, the content expression remaining on his face. "Of course I want kits. But I am content to wait until you are ready to fulfill resonance."

"And how much longer is that? How long can we go?" Already I feel like my cootie gets louder and more insistent every day. Even now, I can hear the thrum of his so urgently that I wonder it isn't shaking his entire body with the force of its song.

He looks thoughtful. "Jo-see and Haeden managed to last a turn of the moon...but they were separated for much of it."

An entire month? The thought seems awful. It's already been weeks and I feel needy and restless, and touching is starting to become less effective. I slide down against him again, my hand on his chest, over his heart. "What if we fulfill it tonight?"

He goes still. "You are ready for that?"

"I don't know if I am or not," I admit honestly. "But I trust you, and I love you, and I ache as much as you do." My hand moves lower, caressing the plates that run along his chest and disappear around his belly button. "And I love it when you touch me. So I think resonance won't be a bad thing."

"There will be kits," he tells me, and puts a hand on my belly. "You have never said how you feel about that."

"It's not something I've ever considered." I put my hand over his. "For so long, I was a slave, and I couldn't think further than the next day or I'd go crazy. It was about surviving, no more than that." I smile at him, loving his brave, strong face. "But I'm starting to think ahead. Slowly. And I think you would be a good father."

There's a look of pure joy on his face that tells me that I'm right. He's going to be a fantastic father, and I'm going to love every moment of watching him with our child.

His arms go around my waist, and he pulls me against him. "Then you wish to do this?"

I pull back and study him, pretending to think about it. Pretending like my cootie's not singing a mile a minute and I'm not hot with need. Pretending like I haven't wanted to rip his leather loincloth off of him for the last few hours. Truth is, I'm a little anxious about going all the way, but there's no one else I'd want to touch me, ever. And I love Bek. I love his caresses and his kisses and when he puts his mouth on my most sensitive spots. Just thinking about it makes my nipples harden. I let my fingers trail over his shoulders, down the center of his chest, and then farther down, to his belly button. I can see his breathing quicken as my fingers go lower and I tug at the ties of his loincloth. "I want you," I tell him. "I want you, and I want this. I don't want to be scared of anything that happens between us."

Bek slides one hand up my arm and then sits up. He cups my face in his hands and kisses me. "Never be afraid of anything we have together, my mate. I would never hurt you."

I know that. I'm not afraid of him. I'm more...afraid of the unknown, just like I was with touching myself.

Of course, that turned out amazing.

It's time to stop being afraid. So I grab him by the mane and pull his face to mine, kissing him with all the bottled-up passion of weeks without fulfilling resonance.

He hesitates, but only for a moment. Then he's grabbing me and pulling me under him, his weight pressing over me as we continue to kiss and roll about in the furs. There's no fear in me, only eagerness and excitement. I want this. I want him. I'm gasping between kisses as his tongue strokes mine, promise in every slick movement. Those ridges along his tongue rub in a delicious way, and I remember what it's like when he uses them on me...lower. A little moan escapes my throat.

"My mate," Bek groans, pressing hot little kisses to my jaw and then to my throat. "You have no idea how long I have wanted this." He begins to kiss lower, his mouth moving to my collarbones.

And even though I want to be brave and enjoy this, I start to get nervous. I remember all the terrible things I'd seen back in the slave cages, the eyes that looked at me with lust even when I was young or very dirty, and the fear I had. It makes me stiffen a little, makes my enthusiasm die a bit. I don't want to think about this stuff. I don't. But I can't help it.

Bek senses my mood change and sits up, giving me a concerned look. "Ell-ee?"

"I'm sorry," I say quickly. "I'm fine." And I put my arms around his neck.

His expression grows angry, and his hand goes to my chin. He forces me to look him in the eye. "Apologizing, are we?"

I am. Ugh. "I want you. I do. My brain is just...going to bad places." I feel frustrated and unhappy at the thought. I want to enjoy this. I love Bek. We've kissed and cuddled so many times in the past. Why won't my brain play along?

"Look at me," he murmurs, voice hot and calm and somehow soothing. I look at him, even though it feels hard, like I'm disappointing him. But his gaze is steady and firm, and the hand on my chin is unyielding. "Am I safe?"

I lick my dry lips. "Safe," I whisper, agreeing. And I feel a little better the moment the word leaves my mouth. Just saying it aloud confirms it. This is Bek. He's safe.

"Do you trust me to give you pleasure?"

I can't help but squirm a little at that. The intense look on his face is making me feel breathless with both nerves and anticipation. "Yes."

He takes my hand in his and kisses my palm, his lips gently brushing over the soft skin. "Then give yourself over to me.

Trust me to pleasure you." At my little nod, he takes my hand and places it atop my head, on my pillow. "Do not move that from there."

Keep my hand above my head? I frown a little at how odd it seems. But when he takes my free hand and places it next to the other, I realize what he's doing. He's giving me something to hold on to and at the same time taking the control from my hands. If I'm clutching my pillow, I'm lying back and letting him pleasure me.

The thought is both erotic and a little intimidating.

"Can I touch you?" I whisper. I love the feel of his skin against mine.

"Next time," he says, and begins to pull apart the laces on my tunic. "There will be many times in the future, my sweet mate. But this time, I am going to do everything, and you are going to simply enjoy."

I squirm, clutching at my pillow. "C-can I help you take my clothes off?"

"No. This gives me pleasure." His voice is so firm and authoritative that it makes me feel all hot and breathless. I watch as his big fingers move down the laces, loosening them until the neck of my tunic is completely open. He tugs the laces off and then tosses them aside and gently peels apart the sides of my tunic. I'm reminded of the last time he went down on me, when he very gently—and very intently—parted my folds and then moved in to lick me. Maybe it's because I'm imagining that, but I'm panting by the time he leans in and lightly kisses the tip of one breast and then the other.

And oh god, do my nipples ache for more.

"My sweet, sweet mate," he tells me again, voice a low, husky rasp. "Look at your perfect little teats. Your beautiful soft skin. I want to lick every inch of you."

I tremble at his words, because he has licked every inch of me, but I still love the thought of him doing it all over again.

He strokes a thumb over my nipple, rubbing back and forth until the already-stiff peak is so tight and aching I can scarcely breathe. My skin prickles with awareness, and when his hand moves to the other breast, I'm practically pushing it into his grip. My fingers dig into the pillow under my head as he lowers his mouth to one breast and teases the other with his hand. The sound that escapes me is a choked, breathless gasp, and my cootie feels as if it's on fire, it's vibrating so strong. It's like I have an earthquake in my chest, and the constant shiver of it is just adding to the arousal I feel in my tight nipples.

I watch breathlessly as his tongue swirls over one tip, and then he nips it gently with his teeth.

I can't bite back the moan that rises in my throat, and I release the pillow to grab at the proud arch of his horns.

"No," he murmurs in that firm voice that makes me wet, and guides my hands back to the pillow. "These stay there. Trust me."

"Safe," I whisper, agreeing. I'm giving myself over to him, and it makes me feel vulnerable and open. Even when I was a slave, there was a part of myself that I always kept locked away behind my silences. With Bek, there's nothing to hide any longer.

He laps at my breasts, teasing them for a bit longer, until I'm shuddering and making small cries. He cups them again, teasing the tips, and then begins to kiss lower on my belly.

"Look up at the stars, my mate," he tells me in a delicious voice. "Watch them as I give you pleasure."

I moan again and force myself to tilt my head back, to watch them instead of him. High above the four stone walls of the hut, the gorge walls rise. Beyond them, the hills that frame the valley. And higher up, the stars. It's a slice of night high above, midnight peppered with greens and reds of distant star systems, sprinkled with the diamond lights of a hundred thousand stars. It's so beautiful, so freeing.

So...distracting. Because now he's untying the lacings on my leggings and tugging them down my hips, and I want to watch, want to see his tongue dip down to lick my folds, to see him bury his face in my warmth and lick me until I'm screaming.

And instead, I'm staring up at the stars.

"Such soft skin," my mate murmurs as he nips at my hip. "But you are still far too thin, my mate. I'm going to stuff you with food until you're plump and pink and rounded."

I giggle at the image. "I don't know if you want me round as a barrel."

He tugs the leathers off my legs, and then I'm naked from the waist down. "I want you round or thin. I want you dirty or clean. I want you every possible way imaginable, my Ell-ee. In my eyes, you are the most desirable thing I have ever seen."

Bek's words take my breath away, as does the gentle kiss he then presses on the inside of my thigh. I whimper and clutch at my pillow as he begins to kiss higher and rests my calf over one shoulder, a big hand bracing my hip. Oh, I know what's coming next. And oh god, I like it so, so much.

I'm moaning my excitement as he continues to kiss his way to the apex of my thighs. By the time he spreads my folds apart,

I'm so full of pent-up anticipation that I practically explode when I feel his breath on me. But his mouth only hovers. "Are you wet for me?" he asks, and I can feel each word on my sensitive flesh. "Or do I need to lick you until your cunt is so juicy it will coat my cock when I rub it against you?"

I just bite down harder on the pillow, not trusting that I'll be able to make coherent words at the moment.

He chuckles. "I think I shall find out for myself." And with that, he gives me the first lick. Oh god, his tongue, those ridges, his heat...I'm lost. I pull the pillow to my face and bite down on it to muffle my cries as he begins to drag his tongue over me just the way I like, slow and steady. We've done this several times since we've started touching each other, but it never gets old. Never, never. In fact, it might get better with each time, because I know what to expect when his tongue flicks over my clit, or when he pushes a finger deep inside me. The anticipation only adds to the pleasure, and within a matter of minutes, I'm panting and straining, desperate for more.

Bek groans then licks me again. "Never have I tasted anything better. I am addicted to your cunt, Ell-ee. To these pink folds and the sweetness you make for me. You are so wet." His finger slides in and out of me, pumping, and I can hear just how wet I am. And instead of making me embarrassed, it makes me even more turned on. "My cock aches to be inside you, to fill you up."

I whimper. "Want that, too."

"Come for me," he commands me. "Then I'll take you and make you mine."

I want to. I hold the pillow tight as he licks me again, his tongue circling against my clit. Did I think my cootie was loud before? It's nothing compared to the noises it's making now—or maybe that's me. It's hard to tell at this point. All I know is that I'm lost, and Bek's tongue is my only anchor to sanity...and the very thing that's driving me to insanity.

Then, like the snap of a rubber band, I'm coming. Everything in my body tenses, and I gasp, feeling myself clench around the finger he has deep inside me. Pleasure unfurls through my body, and it's the most wonderful, delicious thing. I'm falling, falling, falling, but Bek will catch me. I ride the sensual waves as they roll over me, and when I finally come back to myself, I'm breathless, boneless, and so content.

My Bek moves over me, and then he's kissing me so sweetly, his tongue sliding against my lips, and I can taste myself on him. It gives me a little thrill deep inside me, and I release the pillow I've been twisting to pieces and hold him close. His hand goes to my hips, and then he shifts his weight until he's on top of me, his cock cradled against the apex of my thighs.

"My mate," he whispers, then rubs his nose against mine. "How do you feel?"

"Good," I tell him shyly. Any fear I had is gone, completely licked away by his magic tongue. I give him another kiss and then moan when he takes his cock in hand and rubs it up and down my folds. Then he positions himself at the entrance to my core and leans in to kiss me again. I cling to him, greedy for more, when he pushes himself slowly into me.

I gasp against his mouth, because everything feels different. It's tight and strange and wonderful all at once. He feels incredibly large against me—inside me—but I trust Bek.

"Tell me if this pains you," he tells me, voice raspy with tension. "I go as slowly as I can."

"I'm fine." And I am. It does feel tight and slightly uncomfortable, but I love the intense look that's come over his face, the possessiveness I see in his eyes. I'm loving being possessed by him. So I stroke my hand up and down his arm and make soft, encouraging noises. If this is what he needs to come, I want to give it to him. I've already had my pleasure.

He pushes all the way in, and I can't resist a slight whimper of discomfort. He freezes over me then caresses my cheek.

"My mate. I am sorry." Bek sounds upset.

"What is this, apologies?" I tease him, my voice a little tight. It feels...well, it feels like I'm being invaded, and I'm not entirely sure I like it. My cootie does, though—it's going at full tilt.

"Relax," he tells me, still stroking my cheek and gazing down at me. "We will not move until you are ready."

I nod and touch his arm, feeling the flick of his tail move back and forth. He's pressed so deeply into me that the sensation stops feeling invasive and begins to feel...fascinating. The hollow aching need I normally feel when aroused is gone, and I kind of love the weight of his big body over me. It makes me feel small and protected, and I'm enveloped in his warmth and his scent. I sigh happily after a moment. I like this.

"Better?"

At my smile, he leans in and kisses me again, and shifts his hips, rocking them against me. It feels...interesting.

"Put your legs around me," he murmurs against my mouth.

I nod and do so, and he slides a hand under my ass, tilting me against him. He pulls back and then strokes into me. I smother my gasp, because that feels unlike anything I've ever felt before. And I think I want to feel it again.

"You are frowning," Bek tells me, going still over me. "Hurts?"

"Just figuring it out."

"Then tell me if you wish for me to stop," he murmurs, and thrusts again. My hips move with the force of his body, and he pumps into me again and then begins a slow, steady rhythm. And it's, oh, it's different. It feels like he's pushing and moving against me in ways I've never felt before. He shifts his body again and moves my hips, tilting them just a little more with his next thrust—

And then I feel everything.

I suck in a breath, shocked at the spiral of pleasure that surges deep within my core.

"Like that?" At my jerky nod, he grins and begins to move again. I'm liking this now. I raise my hips with his, transfixed by the glide of his cock inside of me. In, out, in out, and how each time he thrusts into me it feels better than the last.

I claw at his shoulders, urgency rising with every movement. "Bek—I need—"

He takes my mouth in a hard kiss, and my pleasure ratchets up another notch. Yes. I need that. I need all of this.

As our mouths lock, he thrusts into me, harder and deeper, until I can't control myself. I'm making little noises with every push into my body, every rock of our hips, every delicious slam of his cock inside me. I'm so full of need I feel like I'm about to crawl out of my own skin, and still I can't quite reach the peak to get there. I'm panting his name, over and over, and he's moving faster over me, our khuis singing so loudly that it's nothing but an endless buzz in my ears.

"My Ell-ee," Bek grits out, one hand going to cup the side of my face. His eyes lock with mine, his thrusts becoming rougher, less controlled. "My mate."

It's when we lock eyes that I come again. I can feel my walls clench and grip him tight, my body locking around him, and I cry out his name. He presses his forehead to mine, a low growl in his throat as his hips jerk against mine, and I think he's coming, too. Then the pleasure takes over, and there's no more thinking, only feeling. It's the most incredible thing ever.

I'm Bek's and he's mine.

Later on, when we've slid apart, I rest my cheek on his chest and gaze up at the stars. They look the same as they did earlier, which seems funny to me, because I feel like my world has changed again. This time, for the better, of course, but still a change. My cootie's still purring, but it's a little muted, and I press a hand to my chest. "I thought this was supposed to stop when we had sex?"

Bek pulls me against him like I'm a doll and cradles my body against him. He buries his face in my neck and begins to kiss my skin, making my cootie—and the rest of me—wake up again. "It takes a few times. Once you are carrying my kit, it will stop."

"Oh." I trail a hand through his hair, thinking. "Will the sex still be as good?"

He chuckles. "Always."

"Then I'm good with that." I smile up at the stars as he begins to kiss my breasts. I'm good with everything, I think.

EPILOGUE

BEK

"Do those two ever stop?" At my side, Ell-ee wrinkles her nose, her hand on her spear. We walk along the edge of one of the high cliffs, avoiding the deep snows in the valley. Nearby, there is a sheet of ice—something that Ell-ee and the humans call a glacier—and we skirt carefully around it in our journey.

"Never," I say, irritated at the sound of Kate and Harrec bickering from behind us. I shake my head. "They both need to be muzzled."

She giggles, the sound light, and it fills me with as much joy now as it did the first time I heard it. My Ell-ee is a quiet one, but around me, she talks. Around me, she smiles. And around me, she laughs. Her joy is slow to unfurl around others, but she trusts me.

It is a precious gift and one I do not take for granted.

She slips her hand into mine, fingers interlocking. She's taken off her glove so she can hold my hand, and I will chide her about it, but later. For now, I enjoy that she wishes to touch me as much as I enjoy touching her.

It has been a full turn of the moon since we fulfilled resonance. My khui has calmed, for the most part, but still sings with joy whenever my mate is near. It did not take us long to finish our resonance—we mated several times that first night, and by the morning, I knew Ell-ee carried my kit. The thought fills me with pleasure and terror all at once, and I hold her hand a little tighter as we walk. The great cold snowstorm came, just as Rokan predicted, and for nearly two hands of days, the world was bitterly, unusually cold. Ell-ee and I bundled up under the roof of our new hut and kept to the furs, learning each other and enjoying the other's company.

Now that the weather has cleared again, we are taking the long hike across the land to where the Elders' Cave is. The ship rests on its belly once more, and Har-loh and Mardok have been working there through the entire bitter season to get things working as they did before. We are escorting the new humans there so they can get the sa-khui language put into their minds by the com-pew-tor. I did not like the idea of taking my delicate Ell-ee on such a long walk, but she was excited about the prospect of seeing so much of the world.

And I can deny her nothing.

Now I see my fears were for nothing. My Ell-ee is a fierce spirit, and she handles the endless hiking better than the other humans. Ahead of us, Vaza carries Chail on his back like a child. Taushen and Warrek take turns pulling the sled with the two chattering humans Brooke and Suh-mer. Sessah scouts ahead for our small group, and Harrec and Kate take up the rear behind myself and Ell-ee.

And they bicker.

And bicker.

And bicker.

I do not know why Harrec needles the female so much. He has confessed to me by the fire that he likes her, even if she does not return the affection. "I will wear her down," he told me with a grin last night. "She will like me eventually. She just needs to realize I am the right hunter for her. If you see that we have fallen behind the group, do not bother to come looking for us. I will leave behind a boot so you know it was on purpose, and then I will entice Kate into my furs. I will bring her back once her heart is mine."

I just rolled my eyes at that and ignored it. He cannot carry that one off, I think. Kate would plant a fist in his jaw and fight him every step of the way, and she is the only human female close in size to a sa-khui female. Harrec does not seem to mind that he has not resonated to any of the females, deciding that he will woo the strong-willed Kate even if she dislikes him. The other males are less easy to understand. Taushen, once cheerful and upbeat, has become more moody and withdrawn. Warrek is Warrek, always calm and quiet, thoughts kept to himself.

Resonance will decide at some point for them, I hope. If not, it is as my Ell-ee says. I cannot make it happen for them.

I take one of the travel cakes out of my pocket and take an absent bite out of it, then hand it to my mate. "Tired?"

She takes the food from my hand and begins to eat. "Not at all. The suns are still high in the sky. Plenty of hours to travel yet."

"Mm. And your stomach?" I am waiting for her to get ill. Norah is already sick to her stomach with her new kit, sending poor Dagesh scrambling for more stomach-soothing tea leaves at every opportunity. My Ell-ee has shown no signs of such illness, but I watch her closely just in case.

"Fine." She finishes the cake and licks her fingers. Behind us, the argument between Kate and Harrec grows to a fever pitch. It seems that the more Kate protests, the more Harrec laughs at her, which just makes her angrier.

I shake my head at their nonsense. If Harrec thinks this is how he woos a female, he needs lessons.

We continue walking for a time, and I am lost in thought. I taste another cake and give it to Ell-ee. I want to keep my mate—and my kit—well-fed. "How many more days until we get to the spaceship?" she asks. Ell-ee's eyes are bright with enthusiasm.

"Another hand of days. You should pace yourself." I put a hand on her light pack—because I will not let her carry more—and nudge it. "I can carry this."

She rolls her eyes at me, full of fire. "You can carry it tomorrow. Maybe." She tilts her head and gives me a teasing look. "Depends on how tired I am tonight."

There is a promise in those words, and I imagine another night by the fire, touching furtively under the furs so as not to get the attention of the others. I do not think we are good at hiding what we do. I also do not think my Ell-ee cares, not when I touch her between her thighs. She is insatiable, my mate. I grin at her. "I will make you very tired."

"Then tomorrow," she promises, and her brows draw together in a little crease as she gazes forward.

I look, and the others walking along the ridge have paused. Warrek moves toward us in lanky, graceful motions, his long mane fluttering in the wind.

"What is it?" I ask as he approaches.

He nods at us, and Ell-ee falls silent. She is still quiet around others, though she occasionally speaks now to Chail or Claire. In time, she will perhaps speak more with the others. Perhaps not. As long as she is content with her silence, I do not mind if I am the only recipient of her words.

"They are gone," Warrek says, and gestures behind us.

I glance backward. Kate and Harrec are gone indeed, no trace of them veering off of our path behind us. I do not know how I managed to ignore their endless screeching, but it seems I have. "Fools."

"Should we look for them?" Warrek asks, concern on his face. "Could they be injured?"

I think of Harrec's boasts to me. If he has taken Kate off somewhere, it is because she wished to go. No one could take that female anywhere she did not want to go. And he said he would court her. Perhaps their bickering leads to mating, like Raahosh and his Leezh. "Harrec said that if they left the trail, not to follow them."

"Mm." Warrek crosses his arms over his chest, concerned. "I do not like it. Perhaps we should look for them."

"Or for a boot," I say, remembering Harrec's words from last night.

Our small group scatters and backtracks. It does not take long to find a boot. Ell-ee holds it up, brows wrinkled with concern. I just shake my head. It seems the males in our tribe all want to take a mate the hard way. First Raahosh when he stole Leezh, then Hassen when he stole both sisters. Me when I forced Ell-ee and her companions to come here. Will no one ever learn?

But as I pull my mate close and press a kiss to her forehead, I think about what I gained. My precious, beautiful Ell-ee.

I suppose they will never learn. Not when the rewards are so magnificent and bring so much happiness. "Let us head on to the Elders' Cave. Harrec and Kate will catch up with us."

AUTHOR'S NOTE

You guys know Bek was never supposed to have a book, right? ;)

Of course, I never really planned on writing past the first few unless things took off. Boy, have they taken off. Suddenly I'm running out of tribespeople and everyone's resonating and getting stories and...Bek's been waiting this whole time. He's got the biggest fan club and I can't thank my Facebook fans enough for constantly encouraging me to write his book. You guys wanted to see him happy, and I loved writing this book. LOVED.

I know a lot of people out there wanted Bek with a ball-buster, but I think Elly works perfectly for him. Sometimes the strongest ones are the quietest, unbroken ones.

Of course, this means we're setting up for a few more books! We've got new ladies in the tribe, a few single bachelors as of yet, and a whole mess of families to play with. I've had a lot of people ask me if we're done with barbarians.

Not done. Not done unless you guys stop buying them. :)

If sales go in the toilet, it tells me that it's time to move on. Until then, I'm just as happy to write them as ever! When we run out of tribespeople, if sales are still strong, we'll maybe revisit some existing couples (I hear a lot of love for Rukh/Harlow, or Josie/Haeden out there) or we'll follow the next generation.

As always, I want to thank my wonderful fans. It's your enthusiasm that keeps me going on bad days, and our mutual love for this tribe that motivates me EVERY day.

Special shoutout to Gabriella, who made a wonderful tribal genealogy chart that I tried to include in this book, but it was so tiny it was unreadable. You can download it on my Facebook page if you haven't yet!

A second special shoutout to readers Becky S. and Julie R. for having my back recently on a hairy little issue that cropped up. All the hearts heading in your direction. <3 <3 <3

And another shoutout to Kati Wilde, who continues to blow me away with every cover. I love this one so much.

The next book is (of course) Kate and Harrec. Will the tribe goofball win his ladylove? Will she put up with his shit? Will he pass out at the sight of his own blood again? Their book's going to be a funny one, I think!

Much love, and thank you for reading. <3

Ruby

ICE PLANET BARBARIANS - THE TRIBE

As of the end of Barbarian's Redemption (8 years post-human arrival)

Mated Couples and their kits

Vektal (Vehk-tall) – The chief of the sa-khui. Mated to Georgie.

Georgie – Human woman (and unofficial leader of the human females). Has taken on a dual-leadership role with her mate.

Talie (Tah-lee) – Their first daughter.

Vekka (Veh-kah) – Their second daughter.

Maylak (May-lack) – Tribe healer. Mated to Kashrem.

Kashrem (Cash-rehm) - Her mate, also a leather-worker.

Esha (Esh-uh) – Their teenage daughter.

Makash (Muh-cash) — Their younger son.

———

Sevvah (Sev-uh) – Tribe elder, mother to Aehako, Rokan, and Sessah

Oshen (Aw-shen) – Tribe elder, her mate

Sessah (Ses-uh) - Their youngest son

———

Ereven (Air-uh-ven) Hunter, mated to Claire

Claire – Mated to Ereven

Erevair (Air-uh-vair) - Their first child, a son

Relvi (Rell-vee) – Their second child, a daughter

———

Liz – Raahosh's mate and huntress.

Raahosh (Rah-hosh) – Her mate. A hunter and brother to Rukh.

Raashel (Rah-shel) – Their daughter.

Aayla (Ay-lah) – Their second daughter

———

Stacy – Mated to Pashov. Unofficial tribe cook.

Pashov (Pah-showv) – son of Kemli and Borran, brother to Farli, Zennek, and Salukh. Mate of Stacy.

Pacy (Pay-see) – Their first son.

Tash (Tash) – Their second son.

Nora – Mate to Dagesh. Currently pregnant after a second resonance.

Dagesh (Dah-zhesh) (the g sound is swallowed) – Her mate. A hunter.

Anna & Elsa – Their twin daughters.

Harlow – Mate to Rukh. Once 'mechanic' to the Elders' Cave. Currently pregnant after a second resonance.

Rukh (Rookh) – Former exile and loner. Original name Maarukh. (Mah-rookh). Brother to Raahosh. Mate to Harlow.- Father to Rukhar.

Rukhar (Roo-car) – Their son.

Megan – Mate to Cashol. Mother to Holvek.

Cashol (Cash-awl) – Mate to Megan. Hunter. Father to newborn Holvek.

Holvek (Haul-vehk) – their son.

Marlene (Mar-lenn) – Human mate to Zennek. French.

Zennek (Zehn-eck) – Mate to Marlene. Father to Zalene. Brother to Pashov, Salukh, and Farli.

Zalene (Zah-lenn) – daughter to Marlene and Zennek.

Ariana – Human female. Mate to Zolaya. Currently pregnant. Basic school 'teacher' to tribal kits.

Zolaya (Zoh-lay-uh) – Hunter and mate to Ariana. Father to Analay.

Analay (Ah-nuh-lay) – Their son.

Tiffany – Human female. Mated to Salukh. Tribal botanist.

Salukh (Sah-luke) – Hunter. Son of Kemli and Borran, brother to Farli, Zennek, and Pashov.

Lukti (Lookh-tee) – Their son.

Aehako (Eye-ha-koh) –Mate to Kira, father to Kae. Son of Sevvah and Oshen, brother to Rokan and Sessah.

Kira – Human woman, mate to Aehako, mother of Kae. Was the first to be abducted by aliens and wore an ear-translator for a long time.

Kae (Ki –rhymes with 'fly') – Their daughter.

Kemli (Kemm-lee) – Female elder, mother to Salukh, Pashov, Zennek, and Farli. Tribe herbalist.

Borran (Bore-awn) – Her mate, elder. Tribe brewer.

Josie – Human woman. Mated to Haeden. Currently pregnant for a third time.

Haeden (Hi-den) – Hunter. Previously resonated to Zalah, but she died (along with his khui) in the khui-sickness before resonance could be completed. Now mated to Josie.

Joden (Joe-den) – Their first child, a son.

Joha (Joe-hah) – Their second child, a daughter.

Rokan (Row-can) – Oldest son to Sevvah and Oshen. Brother to Aehako and Sessah. Adult male hunter. Now mated to Lila. Has 'sixth' sense.

Lila – Maddie's sister. Once hearing impaired, recently reacquired on *The Tranquil Lady* via med bay. Resonated to Rokan. Currently pregnant for a second time.

Rollan (Row-lun) – Their first child, a son.

Hassen (Hass-en) – Hunter. Previously exiled. Mated to Maddie.

Maddie – Lila's sister. Found in second crash. Mated to Hassen.

Masan (Mah-senn) – Their son.

Asha (Ah-shuh) – Mate to Hemalo. Mother to Hashala (deceased) and Shema.

Hemalo (Hee-muh-low) – Mate to Asha. Father to Hashala (deceased) and Shema.

Shema (Shee-muh) – Their daughter.

———

Farli – (Far-lee) Adult daughter to Kemli and Borran. Her brothers are Salukh, Zennek, and Pashov. She has a pet dvisti named Chompy (Chahm-pee). Mated to Mardok.

Mardok (Marr-dock) – Bron Mardok Vendasi, from the planet Ubeduc VII. Arrived on *The Tranquil Lady*. Mechanic and ex-soldier. Resonated to Farli and elected to stay behind with the tribe.

———

Bek – (Behk) – Hunter. Brother to Maylak. Mated to Elly.

Elly – Former human slave. Kidnapped at a very young age and has spent much of life in a cage or enslaved. First to resonate amongst the former slaves brought to Not-Hoth. Mated to Bek.

Unmated Elders

———

Drayan (Dry-ann) – Elder.

Drenol (Dree-nowl) – Elder.

Vadren (Vaw-dren) – Elder.

Vaza (Vaw-zhuh) – Widower and elder. Loves to creep on the ladies. Currently flirting with Gail.

Unmated Hunters

———

Harrec (Hair-ek) – Hunter.

Taushen (Tow – rhymes with cow – shen) – Hunter.

Warrek (War-ehk) – Tribal hunter and teacher. Son to Eklan (now deceased).

Former Human Slaves

Gail – Divorced older human woman. Had a son back on Earth (deceased). Approx fiftyish in age. Allows Vaza to creep on her (she likes the attention).

Kate – Human female. Extremely tall with white-blonde curly hair. Likes to argue with Harrec.

Brooke – Pink-haired human female. Former hairdresser.

Summer – Human female. Tends to ramble in speech when nervous.

ICE PLANET BARBARIANS READING LIST

Are you all caught up on Ice Planet Barbarians? Need a refresher? Click through to borrow or buy!

Ice Planet Barbarians – Georgie's Story
Barbarian Alien – Liz's Story
Barbarian Lover – Kira's Story
Barbarian Mine – Harlow's Story
Ice Planet Holiday – Claire's Story (novella)
Barbarian's Prize – Tiffany's Story
Barbarian's Mate – Josie's Story
Having the Barbarian's Baby – Megan's Story (short story)
Ice Ice Babies – Nora's Story (short story)
Barbarian's Touch – Lila's Story
Calm - Maylak's Story
Barbarian's Taming – Maddie's Story
Aftershocks (short story)
Barbarian's Heart – Stacy's Story
Barbarian's Hope – Asha's Story
Barbarian's Choice – Farli's Story
Barbarian's Redemption – This book!

Next up...

Barbarian's Lady (Kate's Story)

FIRE IN HIS BLOOD

Ruby does dragons! Have you tried it yet? Click on the cover to borrow!

YEARS AGO, THE SKIES RIPPED OPEN AND THE WORLD WAS

DESTROYED IN FIRE AND ASH. DRAGONS - ONCE CREATURES OF LEGEND - ARE THE ENEMY. VICIOUS AND UNPREDICTABLE, THEY RULE THE SKIES OF THE RUINED CITIES, FORCING HUMANITY TO HUDDLE BEHIND BARRICADES FOR SAFETY.

CLAUDIA'S A SURVIVOR. SHE SCRAPES BY AS BEST AS SHE CAN IN A HARD, DANGEROUS WORLD. WHEN SHE RUNS AFOUL OF THE LAW, SHE'S LEFT AS BAIT IN DRAGON TERRITORY. SHE ONLY HAS ONE CHANCE TO SURVIVE - TO SOMEHOW 'TAME' A DRAGON AND GET IT TO OBEY HER.

EXCEPT THE DRAGON THAT FINDS HER IS AS WILD AND BRUTAL AS ANY OTHER...AND HE'S NOT INTERESTED IN OBEYING.

WHAT HE IS INTERESTED IN IS A MATE.

WANT MORE?

For more information about upcoming books in the Ice Planet Barbarians, Fireblood Dragons, or any other books by Ruby Dixon, like me on Facebook or subscribe to my new release newsletter. I love sharing snippets of books in progress and fan art! Come join the fun.

As always - thanks for reading!

<3 Ruby